QUIET

as

Kept

Ebook on Kindle & Nook

ISBN: Paperback 9798392616114
ISBN: Hardcover 9798392968152

First Printing Edition 2023

Brittney M. Buchanan Publishing

Instagram: Brittney.M.Buchanan

CONTENTS

To my family & friends that I forced to read my pages well into exhaustion.

Thank you for being there, being honest, and motivating me forward. Love you all!

ONE

THE NIGHTS AT THE ROUND TABLE

Fall 2022 - Los Angeles, California

Mia Edmunds left her apartment at 10pm arriving at the parking deck of her sister Emily's place around 11. She cracked the window of her rented 2023 BMW letting the Los Angeles autumn night breeze flow through the car. It had a sweetness to it of fresh cut grass and car pollution. Mia sat comfortably against the black leather seat, listening to the heavy bass of music in the distance. Her iPhone vibrated causing the pocket of her light pink duffle bag to turn a brief violet hue. She reached for it knowing exactly who it was. The screen read iMessage from Blaine Abbott and she swiped it up to read it.

Blaine Abbott: Did you make it there safely?

He was such a worrier, she thought, but this brought a smile to her face. She liked that he cared.

Mia: Yeah, I'm still sitting in the car. Just about to go up. I'll text you in a few. <3

She waited for Blaine to reply before turning off the engine of the car. The cellphone light reflected on her face in the darkness when she looked in the rear-view mirror. Her normally brown eyes were hazel in the reflection. The phone vibrated again. She turned the keys in the ignition and the blue headlights went dark.

Blaine Abbott: Okay babe. Take care. <3

Mia swiped through her missed text messages from Emily Edmunds and Sophia Hobbes, also known as "The Ladies," while walking through the parking deck and lobby, by the time she looked up she was already on the elevator. The circular PH button on the elevator's panel glowed neon blue. There was a low ding and the metal doors opened. Rich dark wood floors and the LA night skyline met her view. She readjusted the strap on her shoulder and walked into the foyer.

"Mia!" Emily jumped up from the floor and ran down the hallway towards her, fleece pajamas swooshing back and forth.

"It's been way too long!" Emily's arms were outstretched to hug her.

"Girl, you still have those white couches. How do you even keep them clean?"

Mia looked around the living room, the smell of wildflowers from the old country filled the room. Emily's penthouse was modern, with a lot of dark wood, bright white furniture, and colorful accents. There was a full bar off from the kitchen. The living room had floor to ceiling windows with long white automated blackout curtains, a white stone fireplace with a flatscreen tv over its mantel, and a glass staircase with illuminated steps leading to the second floor and the 3 large bedrooms.

"Sophia, you look beautiful as always, my dear." Sophia and Mia's relationship was uncomfortable most days, but after all this time there was some love there."

Emily took Mia's duffle bag, placing it on the couch. Mia's head turned sharply towards the kitchen as she heard a stumble and a clank of glasses. "Who's that?"

"Dinner! I hired a bartender for the evening. I told him to drink as much of the Peach Schnapps from the bar as he could handle. He should be just the right amount of tipsy at this point since it took so long for you to get here." She placed her arms around her waist and squeezed her so tight she tipped over, unbalanced onto one foot. Emily would always hug her like that when they were kids. Mia kissed her forehead then went over to her duffle bag, grabbing a pair of yoga pants and a sweater, and headed to the bathroom to change.

When she returned, Emily had already dimmed the lights and was placing white pillared candles all around the room. Sophia walked behind her lighting each. Mia walked back to the couch and the ladies plopped onto the pillows around the white coffee table in the middle of the living room. The bartender scurried over to the table, his body swaying back and forth with a black tray balanced in hand.

"You get one drop on my floor... and I'll kill you." Emily's stared at the bartender intently as she spoke, then without a pause her pleasant smile returned as she looked upon Mia and Sophia.

The bartender's shaking hand rolled up his sleeve and rubbed antiseptic on his forearm. He placed his arm over the empty wine glass holding the razor blade in the other hand. One clean swipe and fresh blood began to pour from the gash in his arm and into the glass. He was careful while he poured himself into the second glass and then the third. They watched the color of his tanned Cali skin drain from his face and neck to a balmy pale beige. When they were all at mid-level, he grabbed the gauze pressing it hard against the wound. The bartender placed three square black napkins down on the coffee table and the wine glasses on top. After quickly cleaning up his mess he stumbled back to the bar.

"Looks like he overextended his self." Mia laughed.

"Ooooh, he DOES tastes like Peach Schnapps!" Sophia exclaimed! "You know I really didn't believe you."

"I told you; it would be like drinking the real thing." Emily said proudly.

"Mia, how's things with Blaine? You think you're going to, I don't know, turn him soon?"

Sophia tipped her blood-filled glass towards Mia in support of the question.

"I don't know. I'm not sure he's ready for that. I'm not sure I'm ready for that... I mean he's not 100% certain of my... lifestyle."

"You haven't told him?!"

"You know it's not that simple. Greyson was already a vampire when you met him. And.." She paused abruptly looking at Sophia.

"Never mind."

"You're damn right, never mind." Sophia's eyes flashed an infuriated fluorescent green.

"You know I wasn't going to go there. I was just going to say you haven't dated in a while as far as I know."

Sophia hesitated for a moment. "It's hard to let that go of the past."

"If I could do anything to change the past I would." Mia's hand reached across the table and cupped Sophia's.

"Anywayssss Ladies, what are we up for tonight? Any special movie requests?"

"Nothing with vampires, they never get our fangs right."

"Definitely."

"You know you never told us how you met Blaine. You just up and left us after the whole Michael thing."

"Don't say his name... You know, maybe I should head to bed." Sophia started to get up from the floor.

"No, no Sophia, please stay! I'm sorry." Emily reached for her pink robe.

"Listen, Sophia, we cannot change the past. It doesn't make it less painful, but when you're ready to talk, we'll listen. I saved you not because of what happened, but because it was the right thing to do. My blood runs through your veins. We're all we have now."

"You should have let me die." Sophia whispered to herself.

"Ladies! Ladies! Mia, so you left for the mountains, met a mortal, and had a good time...."

They could hear the flickering of the candles in Mia's silence.

"Mia!" Emily snapped.

Mia got up from the floor with her glass. Taking her usual spot on the couch between the large pillows and the arm of the chair. "Ughh... fine."

"So, what mountains? Where did you go?"

"Colorado. But I wasn't sure where I was going at the time. Mich... He was too narcissistic to follow that quickly, but I knew eventually he'd get bored with himself and would come looking for me."

"Islands are ruined for me. So, I started out in the desolate desert towns of Cali."

"Wait, we were in New York back then and you travelled all the way to Cali that same night? HOW?!"

"I took a red eye flight that night. Then a train was the last leg of the way. You'd be surprised what a do not disturb sign, and blackout curtains can do on a train. It didn't take as long as you think."

"I was there for a couple of months until the one day I was riding down route 111 and I felt him. He was so close it felt like he was in my backseat, I almost crashed my damn car."

"I learned how to live out of this duffle bag here." She patted the bag.

"I didn't go back to my hotel that night. I drove to the airport, got another red eye to Colorado and that's where I stayed."

"Alright! Alright! Now about Blaine or shall I say Young, Mr. Abbott Lover Man." She chuckled.

Mia smiled thinking of his smile again. "Well as he would tell it..."

TWO

TOLSTOY'S BOOKSHOP

Fall 2020 - Leadville, Colorado

The dark gray clouds of twilight faded into the black sky of evening over the mountains in Leadville. It was Friday and while most people were headed to the Manchester Bar on Harrison Avenue, Blaine Abbott, the part time bookshop keeper stood under the back awning in the alley of Tolstoy's Bookshop on East 7th Street. He inhaled the chilly Fall air. A mixture of fresh rain, maple leaves, and burning cedar from a nearby wood stove filled his lungs.

He pulled the collar of his black fleece up, covering his ears and neck from the chill, then reached into his pocket pulling out an old pack of cigarettes. His cold hands shook as he cupped them around his cigarette and lighter, protecting them against the wind and drizzle. The flame briefly illuminated his face showing his pursed lips and furrowed eyebrows, then the alley went dark, all except for the orange dot on the end of the cigarette. He hated smoking, but he wanted to calm his nerves for tonight's plan. He couldn't allow his nerves to get in the way.

It had been raining all day and was beginning to pick up again. He inhaled deeply; the cigarette glowed brighter as its white paper drew back. When he finished, he stepped down onto the alley street bending over to dip the lit end of the cigarette in a puddle until it was out. He threw the soggy butt into an open trash can while grabbing a piece of spearmint gum from his other pocket.

He jogged up the two steps and turned the knob of the back door entering the small foyer. Its checkered tiles squeaked under his wet shoes. He placed his fleece on the coat hook next to the door and headed down the long mahogany aisle towards the front of the bookshop. He sat down at the check-out desk facing the large double front doors. The rain continued to pound away on the skylights. He enjoyed the sound the rain made against the windows.

The brick-faced bookshop had been around for fifty years in the little town. From the outside it looked quaint and mediocre. However, once patrons grabbed the ornate curled gold handles, opened the door, and stepped inside they found that the space was truly grand and magical. A grand Sophie chandelier hung above the check-out desk from the second floor illuminating both floors with soft warm light, matching sconces trailed through every aisle. As you walked in a rich red circular Persian rug laid in front of the check-out desk. The mahogany check-out desk was encircled by floor to ceiling matching mahogany bookshelves filled with thousands of books. Each end shelf was separated by an archway that led to the aisles in between.

Creaky mahogany floors ran the length of the bookshop and at the end of the hall stood a black metal spiral staircase that led upstairs to many more bookshelves and the restroom. The upstairs was carpeted in red plush fibers. The black metal railings completed the balcony that was directly across from the grand chandelier. However, the most special place was the sitting area on the first floor found to the right of the last row of bookshelves. A space made for the cozy reader who just wanted to escape life for an hour or two. The sitting area had another large Persian rug colored in cream and gold that sat in front of a brick fireplace, flanked by two brown leather chaise lounge chairs and a long wooden writing table.

Blaine leaned back in the desk chair, enjoying the thrumming sound that the rain made against the roof and skylights when he noticed the stacks of books that needed to be returned to their shelves. He stood grabbing armfuls placing them on the book cart and headed up the aisle to restock them. He was lost in his own world amongst the books and before he knew it, he was placing the last book on the shelf. He was just about to head back to the front of the shop when he picked up a blue bound book lying on the floor. He thumbed the soft pages and found it was a love story set in the old west about an outlawed cowboy who was fighting for the love of the sheriff's daughter. He read a few pages to pass the time and envisioned himself as the outlaw. He felt strong and powerful, just the confidence boost he needed for tonight.

Blaine sadly was anything but strong and powerful. He was a lean and lanky 5'9. His light brown hair shaped in a wispy pompadour would sometimes fall into his eyes if he did not apply the right amount of pomade. The only thing cool about him, he thought, was his old-fashioned style, tapered short box beard, and his smile. He was shy, a literature major, and the kind of guy who traded in his glasses for contacts, but still at times pushes the imaginary frame's bridge up his nose.

The old grandfather clock chimed eight times. Friday nights were normally slow. There were a few regular customers that would come in during the day to see if any new books had arrived. Mr. Berkeley, a surly old man who was always in a rush. Or that older woman that he could never seem to remember her name, but she always smelled like flowers and greeted him with a big smile. Then there was her, Mia. The one he had been waiting for all day, all week. There was an hour left before closing and she still had not shown up. She was the reason for the butterflies in the pit of his stomach.

Mia was majoring in Chemistry at the same college he was attending across town, but she only took night classes, so they barely saw each other when in school. For the past couple of weeks, she would come in every other Friday and would leave with at least one romance novel. Blaine was enamored by her, the confidence in her walk, the way her smile made everything around her glow. The last time she was there she bought a steamy novel where the woman met a man in a giftshop and eventually made passionate love in the giftshop restroom. Blaine only knew this because after she purchased the book he went home that evening, searched the title online, and spent Saturday through Thursday reading it just so he would have something to talk about if she ever gave him the chance. He felt like he knew what she liked at least romantically based on her book choices, but she made him so nervous. Too nervous to ask her out on a date.

He drifted at the thought of her 5'3 stature, short black pixie hair, and plump dark brown lips that were usually tinted by a vibrant red or purple hued lipstick. He was caught in the rhythm of the rain and then the golden bell above the bookshop's door chimed as it opened. Blaine's light brown eyes peered through the bookshelf over the dust covered books looking towards the door. Mia was closing the door behind her. The rain was dripping from her long double-breasted beige raincoat as she closed the soaked umbrella creating small puddles on the floor.

Mia wore a red, gold, and green headwrap, a bun centered on the top of her head. Her raven black baby hair curled softly down the sides of her face, her lips a deep shade of candy apple red. She knew he liked seeing her lips in that color by the way he stared at them when she talked. She unbuttoned her raincoat showing her white spaghetti strapped top and long wrap skirt that matched the color and pattern of her headwrap. She hung her jacket on the coat rack, her brown shoulders sparkled golden under the chandelier's light. She looked over at the check-out desk hoping to see Blaine at the counter, but it was empty. He must be in the back, she hoped, and for a split second she thought about how frustrated she would be to have taken an Uber in the pouring rain only to find that he had gotten off early and Mr. Tolstoy was working in his place.

The floors creaked beneath Blaine's feet as he walked back to the check-out desk. Mia was looking at the new books. He almost couldn't contain how happy he was to see her, how much he wanted to touch her. Mia turned around with a bright smile and headed over to greet him.

"Wet night, isn't it? I mean I love the rain, but it's getting torrential out there." She laughed, still walking towards him, her arms folded together under her breasts lifting her B cup up to look like a C cup.

"My name's Mia. And you're Blaine, right? I think I've seen you around the college?"

"Yee-ah, I've seen you too a-- few times." Blaine stuttered unexpectedly and his cheeks flushed with red. He waited for Mia to look at him like he was a fool and walk away, but she never did. She continued to stare into his eyes and smile.

"I'm surprised to see you out in the rain. Are you looking for a new romance book?"

"Well, sort of. I was aching for this new book, but I don't see it here." She glanced at the pile of new arrivals and then at the front doors. "It's really raining out there... if you're not busy I'd like the company. No one should be alone on a Friday night." Her tone was sincere and direct. Blaine was melting into a puddle of emotions. He couldn't believe she wanted to be around him. He got lost in his thoughts again and his pause was longer than expected. "Yes! Please stay!" He said a little too quickly. Inside he was hitting his forehead repeatedly, face palming at his responses.

They walked down the aisles of the bookshop, re-shelfing old titles and pointing out their favorite authors and books along the way. He could feel the urge to touch her, to bend her over a pile of books, to kiss the softness of her neck, but he refused to think of it so instead he attempted to make small talk.

"What's with all the romance novels? Do you really enjoy them?"

"I do, they make the world seem like such a beautiful and mysterious place when it could can be so dark." She seemed to daydream at the thought. She was beautiful and mysterious to him.

"Have you ever acted out one before?" Blaine asked shyly.

"I wish! I would love a romantic story of my own." Mia skipped ahead of him running her fingertips across books on the shelf then turning around to face him. "To be adored" she sighed "one can only dream of experiencing that someday."

"I'm sure someone adores you. I mean what's not to adore?"

Blaine's palms began to sweat and in his head he said, "This is it." This was the moment he had been waiting for. He knew he had to set his nerves aside and put himself out there. There would be no other chance if he fumbled it now. It's now or never. He took a deep breath and reached for Mia's hands. They stopped in the aisle and while holding both he gently pushed her against the bookshelf. "I can give you that tonight, if you want. Any night, every night. I-- would like to adore you. I mean if that's cool with you, you can say no."

The coolness of the wood shelves pressed into her back. She could feel the spines of the books against hers. She stared into his eyes and let go of his hands, bringing hers to his face. She smiled before planting a passionate kiss on his lips. Mia's hands trailed down Blaine's chest, stopping at the waist band of his pants.

"Can we um?" She pulled at the loop in his brown belt.

"Only if you want to, I never want to offend you. And before we even start, I have a confession to make…" She kissed him again this time long and slow then stepped back waiting for his response.

"I like you, a lot. I was going to ask you out tonight and have been working up the courage ever since I first saw you come into the shop." He said it so quickly that he felt like he would pass out.

She smiled at him tenderly, "The only reason I have been coming here so much was to see you."

They kissed again then Blaine stepped back. He motioned for her to give him one minute. It was now 10pm and the bookshop was finally closed. He headed towards the front doors locking them in. He made his way to the back foyer and dimmed the lights of the chandelier. All the other sconces dimmed at the same time. He checked that the back door to the alley was locked and then went into the storage closet. It only took him ten seconds to rummage through the boxes to find the emergency yellow candles. He took them to the sitting area where the fireplace was already lit and placed them on the tables around the room.

Mia waited patiently for Blaine to come back and when he did, he grabbed her hand and led her to the sitting area.

The candles and fireplace made the room look enchanted. The cream and gold threads in the Persian rug looked even more ornate in the fire's glow. Blaine wrapped his arms around her waist bending slightly to kiss the curve of her neck. She smelled like rose water and he loved inhaling her scent. They moved in a slow circle still embracing, dancing in the dim light.

Mia guided Blaine backwards and he sat down on the chaise lounge. She began to unwrap her long skirt when he motioned for her to keep it on. He loved what she was wearing. She lifted the skirt just enough for him to see the lace black thong she was wearing. She hooked her thumbs to both sides and slowly lowered them down tossing them over to him. He caught them in mid-air and scrunched them up to his nose. His eyes closed tightly as he inhaled her essence. Her scent filled his nostrils, the dampness was intoxicating. He knew that tonight was going to be the only night that he could show her that she was his, and he was hers.

He stood up tossing her panties on the couch. She frantically was unbuttoning his blue button-down shirt while he was unbuckling his belt. He lifted her up placing her gently on the table next to the chair, knocking the books to the floor in a soft thud. The thigh high split in her skirt slid down and pooled around her thighs. He could see a small patch of soft black hair covering her pussy and her loves lips; small, pinkish, and puckered with her glistening love juice.

He unzipped his pants letting them fall to the floor. His dick was bulging hard at the sight of her. He ran his fingers across her folds feeling the warm wetness hit the cool air of the room when he drew back. He rubbed her wetness on the tip of his dick and placed its head at her entry way. He slowly pumped inside her, her shoulders tensed up as her head rolled back and eyes closed tightly, she was holding her breath. He slowed his rhythm down even more. He was in tune with the rain and the breathing of her body.

He wanted to savor this moment with her and didn't want to run the risk of cumming too soon. She noticed his care and loved that about him, his patience, his strong hands gentle enough to touch her body. He made her feel good, feel human. She rocked her hips at the same pace, grinding into him, taking all of him. He knew that this was not just sex with a girl he liked, he was making love to her, and he hoped that she would want him in more ways than just this once they were finished.

He lifted her off the table grinding himself into her while her legs were wrapped around his waist. It was the most intense feeling he had felt with someone. She came in waves of violent convulsions, her juices dripping down his shaft onto his pants. She slid down his body, hypnotized by the smell of his sweat, his heart pumping. She could feel it throbbing inside of her. She let out a low growl as she focused on its beating until he kissed her lips and turned her around. His dick now caressing the crack of her heart shaped ass through her skirt as he walked her towards the bookshelves. He bent her over, her hands firmly placed on the shelf for balance, and lifted her skirt around her waist, its long cloth draped in the front of her exposing her ass.

He centered himself behind her placing one hand on the back of her neck, the other holding her skirt. As he thrusted inside of her, she grabbed his hand that was holding the skirt, interlocking her fingers with his. A faint wet suction sound echoed in the room, each thrust was slow and deep.

Mia dug her fingernails into Keats & King novels tearing the pages as she steadies her trembling body. He's close and the stack of books won't hold them much longer. She cries out in ecstasy, and he with his head tilted back does the same. He falls onto her back, both panting with exhaustion. Blaine whispers I love you into the back of her shoulder and planted kisses across her back. She whispers the same into the hardcover of a Keats novel.

Blaine awoke the next morning, his back and neck stiff from the desk chair. Disoriented about where he was, he winced at the brightness of the sun that beamed in through the skylights. His eyes met the two double doors of the bookshop. Startled, he heard keys jingling on the other side of the door. The door swung open, and a flood of white morning light stung Blaine's eyes blinding him until the door closed.

Mr. Tolstoy walked over to the check-out desk holding two hot cups of black coffee from the local diner. "Boyo! I saw your car in the parking lot. Did you sleep here? He laughed, handing over the coffee cup to him. "You know it's no problem but... You're lucky you're not as old as me or that desk chair would have had you aching this mornin'." The little old Russian man pointed at the wooden chair. "I didn't intend to. I'm not sure what happened, but I'm going to head out. I'll see you next Friday." Blaine wiped the crust from his eye and yawned.

He stood up and started walking towards the double doors and in an almost instant flood of panic he remembered last night's events. "Mia!" He screamed in his head not knowing if she was still sleeping on the chaise lounge in the sitting area. He could not remember if they had gotten fully undressed. The last thing he wanted was for her to be nude and awoken by Mr. Tolstoy.

He turned around on his heels and Mr. Tolstoy who was counting the money in the register glanced up at him. "Forgot something, Boyo?" he said inquisitively.

"Yeah, I forgot my fleece in the back. I might need it during the week. It has been cold lately." Blaine tried to walk as normal, but as quickly as he could until he was out of the line of sight of Mr. Tolstoy. There was something off about him this morning. He didn't think he ever heard Mr. Tolstoy call him "Boyo" it was always, "Young Abbot", but Blaine was in too much of a rush to go home and get in bed that he simply didn't care. He turned the corner to the sitting area. His eyes fell upon the room and his head tilted a little to the side in confusion. The room was exactly the way it was when he began his shift. The books laid neatly on the writing desk. The were no candles and the fireplace had been put out.

His head was pounding, and his mouth was dry. He was not sure if what happened was real or if he just had a pleasant dream. He would not have been so lucky to have been with Mia on the same night as professing his admiration and care for her.

"Well, we can try again next Friday. Hopefully, I didn't fall asleep while she was here. I mean why would I, I wasn't even tired. But if I did, I hope she does not think I'm a total weirdo."

He walked back to the front of the bookshop. Mr. Tolstoy was on his cellphone. He waved a half-handed wave back to him as he pushed the handle on the door and stepped out into the cool autumn sunshine. His beat up 1984 Pontiac Fiero sat in the parking lot, the sun reflecting off its red paint. He opened the car door and sat down on the old, tattered tan seats. He placed his head on the steering wheel and let the cool waxy plastic soothe his warm forehead. His thoughts were running wild, and his self-doubt had begun to consume him. He sat up and placed his keys in the ignition and turned. All he wanted to do was go home and sleep. The engine roared loudly, and a full blast of balmy air came from its vents. As he welcomed the warm air and dropped the car into first gear he suddenly stopped. He took a deep breath through his nose and the faint smell of rose water perfume gently fanned across his face from his button-down shirt.

Emily was walking back from the kitchen; her wine glass had been refilled. Sophia was staring at the blaze in the fireplace.

"So, you WILLINGLY went to college?"

"Yeah, Chem night classes. I wanted to try it out."

"Who does that...." Emily scoffed.

"Oh boy, not for all the immortality in the world." Sophia laughed.

"Exactly, no ma'am."

"It was actually interesting. Honestly, I think it's something I'm going to do from time to time. Keep up with the times, you know. The only downside was having to hunt outside the campus grounds, but other than that it was an experience."

"Wait, wait, so you had sex with him? How did you not bite him during all that heart pumpin' action?!"

"I honestly don't know, Em. I think I focused on the rain or something. I wanted to and was close towards the end, but the morning was coming, and ...there was an emergency, so I put everything back and ran out the back door. I did do a low growling though. I think he was so nervous that he didn't notice."

"Lucky for him I guess."

"You should tell him and turn him. You seem... invested in this one." Emily wanted her sister to finally trust someone, a male someone, that would accept her and love her. Blaine seemed closer than any man she had spoken of besides Michael.

"It's been 2 years, right? And he hasn't noticed you haven't aged? The night only dates? How old is he now?!"

"Emily, too many questions. He's 33 now and MOST dates are at night."

"33 is a perfect age! Tell em' and turn em'. I always wanted a brother."

"We'll see. When I get back I plan on having the conversation, but until I'm in relax mode."

"Alright, alright." Emily let up.

"Excuse me Ms. You never told us about how you and Greyson met? All up in my business... Where is that blue eyed devil anyways?!"

"He was so suave." Emily eyes lowered, glowing golden rings reflecting in the blood in her glass. Sophia remained silent.

"Was?"

"Was..."

"Oh Em..." Mia started to get up from the couch to comfort her, but Emily waved her hand for her to stay sitting.

"It happened while you were gone... It's fine."

"I would have come back had I known. I really am sorry. How did it happen?!"

"He's not dead, I think. Just gone..."

Emily walked over to the window, staring out at the skyline. The twinkling of building lights looked like distant stars on a foreign planet.

"We met at an opera house, in Italy... 1851. And he was so suave."

THREE

———

THE ONLY MAN IN GREY

Emily glanced over the balcony at the audience full of black tailcoats and satin gowns all mingling together under the golden theater house candles. She leaned against the cool metallic railing, her sapphire and diamond bracelet dangling above the crowd as she held an old-fashioned pair of golden binoculars in her gloved hand. She squinted her hazel green eyes through the small lens aiming towards the back rows. Not a familiar face in sight, but she did admire all the beautiful diamonds, rubies, and emeralds glistening on the necks and ears of the rich patrons.

The stage lanterns dimmed. Most people were already seated, except for the last-minute stragglers bumping into knees and stepping on toes in the darkness. Emily's spying was interrupted by a faint cold breeze. It smelled of spiced cologne barely noticeable to the average nose. She closed her eyes for a moment pinpointing the owner and when she opened them his eyes caught her gaze. He was the last man to sit down in the furthest back row. His eyes were iridescently blue like a wolf in the night. When she raised her binoculars to get a closer look, he was already staring at her. "He's got a good eye." she thought to herself. She smirked at him lowering her binoculars, returning her eyes to the stage below. A faint whisper from a male voice invaded her mind "He's... got good ears too." Emily was stunned. She didn't like it when people could read her thoughts.

She raised her binoculars again searching for his face to confront him, but he was gone. The red bellowing curtains rose above the stage as a man dressed in colorful make up and a clown suit stepped his heavy clunky feet across the stage. The violins sprung into a beautiful symphony as the clown pirouetted across the stage.

About an hour into the performance, she felt the arrival of Mia. They always loved seeing the arts together. Luckily, too. The performance had just reached the part where the plush seats had become uncomfortable to sit in. Most of the men in the audience were yawning in unison while their female companions stared wide eyed and stargazed at the heart throb in the ballet tights leaping and professing his love in Italian.

Emily stood up, taking one last look into the crowd for the mystery man before exiting the booth. The singing was silenced to a low hum as Emily walked down the long corridor. At the end of the hall was a large oak door. Emily turned the golden knob and entered the parlor.

"Dessert?" Mia asked looking at the parlor door closing.

"No not tonight. Plus, I think I'll let the mystery man have it."

"Mystery man? You saw another like us?"

"Yup, in the theater just before I met up with you. He's telepathic too so mind what you think." Emily said cautiously. "I lost him before coming in here. He was cute, tall, but arrogant."

"Sounds like my type." Mia laughed as they clinked their wine glasses together.

"Wait!" Sophia interrupted. "You never told me you both went to Italy!"

"It was in 1851. You weren't even born yet."

"But! I'm Italian! Come On!" Sophia raised her arms up like the Italians she saw on the Sopranos, not far from the personalities of some of her past relatives. Then she blurted out.

"Wait, 1851 in Italy, weren't people racist towards you two?"

"Of course!" Emily laughed. "And I glamoured every one of their asses. Those who were particularly rude I fed on. I wasn't as nice as I am now." She looked towards the bar where the bartender stood wiping the dust off three fresh wine glasses.

"Okay, Continueeee!" Sophia urged.

The thought trailed away from Emily's mind as she walked down the corridor. She ran her gloved hand across the golden crown molded walls. The doors and entry ways were all outlined in the same gold. The wallpaper was beautifully intricate damask print, and the floors were speckled cream, gold, and brown. Huge gold rimmed mirrors hung on the wall with chandeliers sconces on each side. The stairs to the theater lobby were white marble. Emily paid close attention to the sound her heels made while walking down the steps alone.

She was enamored by the paintings and sculptures of angels, nude women, and cherubs. It reminded her of the deities of Greece; Aphrodite, Persephone, Hades, and Zeus; ones her and Mia once watched a sculptor create one summer night from the balcony of their chalet in The Acropolis of Athens. This was a time when

Mia and Emily still used their born human names, Malay and Salma.

"Wait! Pause again!" Sophia said. "Malay and Salma?"

"Yeah, when we were humans many centuries ago in Morocco our mother, Zara; a beautiful and powerful high priestess named us after her two sisters, Malay and Salma. Of course, we had to change that to keep up with the times. But we still honor her in other ways." Mia glanced at the white vase full of Moroccan wildflowers.

"Beautiful and so wise, we saw a lot through her eyes." Emily chimed in.

"Now stop interrupting!" Emily glared.

At the end of the lobby was a small gallery. A room of white marble walls and floor where a larger golden vase stood in the middle, dozens of blood red roses protruding from its neck. Her bronze skin was a beautiful contrast in the stark white room. The scene was breathtaking, and then she realized she was not alone.

"Your smell gives you away. It's spiced, nice, but apparent." she said while defiantly touching the antique golden vase on display.

Greyson Bradford gazed lovingly at the back of her dress hugging her 5'5 frame. He wanted to run his hand down the nape of her neck to the small of her back where the dress dipped in. She examined the dust from the vase on her white gloves then turned to face him. He was the tallest man in the room standing at 6'4. She could clearly see his features now, jet black hair, iridescent blue eyes, and a lean gray tailcoat.

"Defiant." he laughed.

"Very." She confidently reassured him.

Emily's heels clicked on the tiles as she walked towards the exit of the gallery.

Without even glancing towards him she whispered seductively. "Take me somewhere special. Now."

Greyson smirked at her boldness. He walked with her to the lobby, placed her white fur coat upon her shoulders, and headed towards the carriage to prepare his driver for a journey.

FOUR

A CABIN IN THE SNOW

Spring 1851 - Selva di Val Gardena, Italy

It was just 2AM when the carriage finally pulled onto the snowy dirt road in Selva di Val Gardena. Emily opened the leather flap that covered the window to feel the cold mountain air on her face. Little flecks of drifting snow caressed her warm cheeks and neck. A small moan escaped her lips at the coolness. She turned to look at Greyson to see if he had heard. When her eyes met his she realized he had already been staring at her. He grinned that devilish grin and gently grabbed her hand squeezing it just enough to make her tremble.

The horses came to a stop and the carriage rocked back and forth as the driver jumped into the snow. The driver gathered two trunks from the storage and then approached the carriage door. Once opened, Emily stretched in the warmth of the plush seat not ready to get out of the cab yet. Greyson stepped out first securing his foot on the carriage step before reaching for her hand. Her white glove gripped his palm and the door frame as she steadied her legs, tired from sitting in the same spot for hours. Emily stepped out onto the soft fresh powder, inhaling deeply the mountain smell once more, admiring the cabin's beauty amongst nature. It was a dark night, but she could see its contrasting pine wood and stone facing against the thick snow-covered mountain backdrop. The giant snow dusted pine trees with hints of emerald-green encircled the cabin, making a complete open window to the sky above as the moonlight beamed onto it. There was a dock far off in the back with a wide solid lake beneath it covered in drifts of snow.

"Do you bring all your guests here?"

"Do we need more guests?" He held her hand firmly as they walked to the cabin door.

"Not yet. But that's not answering my question."

"You're smart too, I like that."

"Answer please." She pulled away gently so he would know she was serious.

"No, just you. You said a special place. This cabin is special to me. It's where I was born."

They entered the grand foyer where Greyson advised the driver to gather wood and start a fire in the large fireplace that sat in the middle of the room. Greyson began lighting candles all around the cabin until the room glowed in a honey hue. Emily stared up at the beams where the small cobwebs hung on the antlers of a grand chandelier. The driver had begun lighting the candles on that too after the fireplace was lit. The room was freezing as if no one had been there in an eternity but had started to warm up. She always hated the cold. There were old blankets of royal blue and deep reds from olden times, some looked even older than Emily, she thought to herself.

There were antiques of all kinds from rugs to urns with dried flowers to stuffed heads of wolves, bears, and mountain lions, and all kinds of hunting tools.

Emily smelled fresh cut wood and dust while walking down the long hallway. She reached a solid pine door with hand carved scrolls embossed on its face and turned the handle. The warmth from the lit fireplace greeted her as she stepped into Greyson's bedroom. There was a king-sized bed made of oak and iron. On each side were night tables where two porcelain urns filled with red roses sat surrounded by candles. The roses from the gallery she thought. She ran her hand across the soft linens, a fluffy black bear skin blanket was draped over the end of the bed. It was a drastic change from the foyer and living area with its rustic bachelor feel.

Greyson's footsteps were coming down the hallway towards the bedroom and in his one hand he was dragging a stone chair from the dining room. It reminded Emily of a Nordic throne. He placed the chair at the foot of the bed and sat down.

Emily's eyebrow raised as she knew what she wanted to do with him. She walked over to her trunk that the driver had brought in and unclasped the golden latch. There were few moments of silence as she shuffled through garments, but then she stood up holding a medium satin black satchel in her hands. Emily reached into the bag and pulled out a triple braided piece of rope. He stared at it, puzzled at first and then he grinned with curiosity and excitement.

She slowly walked around the back of the chair, her hands caressing his shoulders and arms slowly placing his hands behind his back. With speed she wrapped the rope around his wrists and pulled tightly binding them together. He smiled at her attempts at roughness, quickly putting on a serious face when she walked back around the chair to face him. Emily placed a satin blind fold over his eyes and walked away leaving him in anticipation.

Greyson sat there for five minutes while she prepared in the washroom. Emily watched herself in the gold framed mirror undo her opera gown and let it fall into a puddle around her feet. She slowly took off each garment until she was fully nude. Her bronze skin shimmered golden in the candlelight. Once again, she reached for the black satchel, taking out perfume and red lip rouge. She applied light dabs of perfume to her collar bone, in between her breasts, hips, and thighs. With the tip of her finger, she delicately smudged rouge onto her lips and before exiting the washroom she pulled out a red and gold feathered mask placing it over her eyes.

Emily eased back into the bedroom and stood in front of his chair.

"Is the rope too tight?" She whispered in his right ear.

Greyson remained silent and shook his head.

"Good." she said sharply.

He could hear the seductive dominant tone of her voice. She removed his blindfold to see those piercing blue eyes catching the fire's light, eager to adjust to the dimness of the room. Once adjusted, his mouth fell agape as his eyes took in her fully nude body. She watched as his eyes trailed from her bare feet, up her supple calves, thick thighs, toned stomach, juicy breasts, and ending at her plump red lips. Emily's hips swayed as she circled around his chair, her nails becoming sharper with each pass. The flames reflected in her eyes giving a fox lime green hue under her vibrant mask.

Emily kept her eyes locked onto his as she stopped to face him. Her legs spread wide as she lowered herself onto his lap. The heat from her pussy caressed the stiffness in his slacks. A moan hummed from her mouth at his size & hardness. He pounded slowly into her as she kissed him roughly… deeply, taking his bottom lip into her mouth while her hand gently rubbed her wetness below.

She raised her fingers to his lips, the clear liquid slipped between her digits. His tongue tasted her and with a deep guttural moan his eyes closed to savor the taste.

"Good boy." she held the sides of his face.

The ropes twisted around his wrists and his urge to touch her became unbearable. She stood up to move to the bed, where she lay on top of the bear skin. She teased him, opening and closing her knees showing peeks of her pussy to him.

"It's time to play & you're going to watch…"

"...I want you ferocious. I want you desperately. I want you to be teased to the brink of madness..."

"...And when you can't hold on anymore, when the hardness is just about to hurt. I want you to break those ropes."

She moaned this while spreading her legs as far as they could open, her toes pointed to the wood framed ceiling. His eyes widened at the sight of how wet she was. She could see his hands moving behind his back holding onto the rope, its fibers creating red welts in his palms. She pinched her dark brown nipples between her fingers, whimpering at the sensation and when she released, they were hard and pointing towards the ceiling. She caressed down her stomach, back and forth between her breasts and her belly button. Greyson shifted in his chair every time she inched closer and closer to her pussy. Slowly and gently, her fingertips grazed the curls of her pubic hair. She watched the pinkish hue of her nails every so often separate her lips so he could see her tight wet hole.

Greyson let out a low growl as the pressure built up on his wrists as she continued to stroke faster, slipping one finger inside of her hole then pumping in and out. Her moans became louder and less controlled. Her hand was soaked from her juices. She could see the veins in his face and neck begin to bulge and pulse sending her into an orgasmic wave. Her fangs drew out as she tilted her head back, her body convulsing from the cum. In a swift motion the rope snapped into fibers and the throne was flung against the bedroom door.

Greyson stood, fangs erected and eyes glowing at the end of the bed. Emily looked at what was left of the unraveled bundle of rope on the floor and the freshly made hole in the wall from the chair. In startlement, she propped up onto her elbows. Greyson stared at her shifting breast falling forward, a mischievous grin appears upon his face as she crawled to the top of the bed. The blue of his eyes had now become a stark snow white that glowed gold when he looked at the flames in the fireplace. The hunger in them was almost intimidating, but she smiled lustily at the monster she had created.

He grabbed her ankle with one hand sliding her to the end of the bed. Her legs dangled over the edge searching for the floor. She was exhilarated. He wrapped his arms under her ass picking her up to meet his gaze. Her soft bare breasts lay against his dress shirt. Emily looked down upon his chiseled face, the black stubble on his chin. Her face floated above his 6'4 stature.

"Devour me."

Those two words seethed lusty delight. His eyes squinted and the smile was replaced with a confident smirk as if he said to himself, "challenge accepted". She slid down his body as he placed her on the edge of the bed, her legs spread wide displaying her open glistening pussy to him. He licked his lips at the sight — a quick remembrance from the earlier finger tasting. And with the same quickness he placed his hands under her thighs cupping her hips, roughly lifting both of her legs over his shoulders and with one great grunt she was back in the air. Her legs wrapped around his neck and draped down his back.

Her whimpers filled the room as his tongue entered her pussy with precision. The width of his tongue stretched her and caressed each wall. Her juices began to flow down his chin & neck, droplets soaking his clothes. His slurping was intense. Emily's hands dug firmly into his hair pushing his face and tongue deeper into her, her hips ground into his stubble trying to keep the momentum. Her other hand stretched down the back of his dress shirt ripping into the skin of his shoulder. He didn't flinch at the pain. She moaned for him. She screamed for him. Her body quaked & jolted as she came for him.

He threw her onto the bed, body quivering & exhausted. The smell of his blood and her pussy were in the air. She licked her blood dampen hand; her eyes rolled into the back of her head at the taste of his power. She gasped while opening them to see that Greyson was naked and his face was firmly planted in between her thighs. His tongue long and lapping between her lips. She kicked his wounded shoulder and he finally winced in pain and laughter. He climbed up the bed placing himself in between her legs.

Emily grabbed the iron rods in the headboard, bracing herself as he entered her. The iron bent under her grip and for a moment both of their faces morphed into batlike creatures as they roared in the pleasure of her tightness. Emily wrapped her legs around his waist pulling him in deeper while she sank her claws into his back. She could barely see over the muscles of his shoulder, but she could feel the blood dripping over her hands and thighs. Her pussy began to pulse and squeeze his dick, her wetness making his stroke easier to pick up speed. Emily felt another climax coming as he pushed her deeper into the bed. The tingling rose inside of her until she exploded sinking her teeth into his shoulder.

Greyson grunted in pain and ecstasy as he pumped her harder. He came while sinking his fangs into her neck. She screamed and clawed as his blood flowed into her mouth and her blood flowed out of her neck. They pushed each other back to stop the intense thirst, both panting ferociously at opposite ends of the bed. Emily crawled over to him planting a soft kiss on his lips. He grabbed the back of her head kissing her deeply tasting his own blood in her mouth. Her juices and their blood mingled on their tongues. This was the ultimate blood pact... a blood bonding, one neither of them expected would happen that night, one that would bind them forever.

"YOU DID WHAT?! You didn't even know him." Mia was pressing her palm to her forehead in disbelief.

"Leave it alone, Mia. I was young! And I knew he was mine, and from then on he will always be mine... Wherever he is."

"Oh boy. We don't know what could happen to you if something happens to him." Mia could hear Blaine's voice in her words.

"I suppose nothing, but never mind all that. Let's not ruin the night. Who's going next?!"

"I'll go." Sophia raised her hand up like a schoolgirl in class.

"If it will keep you two from bickering the night away about something from 1800 whatever."

"Give me a sec." Sophia got up from the coffee table and headed for the stairs. When she came back, she was holding an old leatherbound diary with a daisy on the front. She tossed it over Emily.

FIVE

FROM SOPHIA, WITH LOVE

Part I: Richard - Crickets in The Night

Winter 1961 - San Jose, California

Richard's wrench tightened the last bolt on the lifted old brown Cadillac's caliper. He reached into the front pocket of his blue coveralls; Lambert's Auto Body embroidered on the pocket in red cursive on a white background, his own name Richard Hobbes was stitched beneath it in the same lettering. He retrieved his neatly folded red handkerchief from the pocket and wiped the sweat from his brow. The stained rag replaced the fine glistening sweat beads with a thin sheen of car smut and goldish brown Pennzoil that blotched the rag from an oil change earlier that day. The smear darkened his caramel-colored skin to a rich brown across his temple.

It was 1961, and an extremely warm summer night in San Jose, California. The body shop stood on Figueroa and Third Street across from Citizen's National Bank and Ralphs Grocery. Richard walked from beneath the car lift, resting his hand on the Cadillac's silver spoked white and black wheel while placing the handkerchief back in his pocket. He glanced down at his watch. It was 7pm, late by his standards.

Richard was 28 years old and had a working man's build from years of farming, lifting tires, and moving heavy beams of metal ever since he was strong enough to help. His rough and calloused hands ran across the short dark curls on his head. His arms and chest were strong and broad which now created a creased snug fit of his coveralls over his shoulders and biceps as he stretched his arms to the ceiling in a yawn. He had one more car to service before he could call it a night, go home to his tv dinner, and empty bed. An empty bed that he longed for only one person other than himself to be in. Richard decided to grab a cold brew and take a break before changing the brakes.

The long beams of white florescent lights hung from the shop's ceiling made the shop feel warmer than the temperature outside the garage.

He had been working in this heat all day and since he was alone on Wednesdays, he wanted to take it easy. He headed to the back room and opened the Frigidaire, grabbing a Budweiser bottle from its ice box. Walking back through the hallway he picked up an empty red milk crate and headed towards the open garage door. He placed the milk crate just outside the entrance. His stocky legs cried out new cracks and aches as he sat down, stretching out his 6'2 frame along the ashen concrete driveway.

He stared out of the open garage door onto the street at the passing cars. He loved California ever since he arrived as a teenager in 1951 from Huntsville, Alabama. California was "alive" as the new age kids would boast, and San Jose was a "groovy" place to be at night, with its shiny new cars that reflected under beautiful bright colored neon signs. It had its rough times, but it was unlike anywhere he had ever seen, and he was enamored by it all.

Richard and his mother moved to California when he was 15 years old, about a year after his father passed away. People from the South states often moved to the West if they could find the means to do as it was a way to find a better life. He missed Huntsville, but knew he would never go back there, and on nights like this as he squinted hard to see what little glimmers of the stars, he could see through the orange streetlights, he would imagine himself as a child sneaking onto the back porch of his grandparent's farm.

He remembered easing out of bed and walking down the dark hallway, attempting to avoid the creaky wood planks beneath his feet. Once he reached the back door, he fumbled with the latch unlocking it then pushing the thin wired screened door open. The full white moonlight wavered across the tall golden wisps of wheat fields that swayed in a melodic dance in the gentle cool country breeze. Over the rumbling loud motors and car radios of the passing Cali cars he could almost hear the coos of nearby crickets singing him those old lullabies while he drifted into a peaceful sleep in his grandmother's old rocking chair.

The sudden bright headlights of a gold Cadillac convertible turning into the autobody's driveway broke his reverie. Richard stood up dusting off his coveralls, not knowing what to expect from the person who was driving the car. The car came to a halt, the engine was silenced, and the lights were turned off. The car door slowly opened and two long legs in sheer red stockings and black kitten heels appeared beneath the door frame. Richard recognized the car and the legs but was worried as to why she would have come there this late in the evening.

His heart pounded as he walked towards her, her legs dangling over the side of the seat. He quickened his pace down the driveway as she never stood up after opening the door. He knew that was not like her as she normally would greet him with a lighthearted happy leap from the car into his arms, especially if no one was around to see it. When he finally reached the driver side of the car, Sophia De Luca's long black hair was in a disheveled bun that rested at the nape of her neck.

Her head leaned up against the driver seat's head rest covering most of her swollen black eye. The orange streetlight reflected off her face and eyes, but you could still see that the whites of her round green eyes were tinted in a reddish hue. She wore a long-sleeved black dress imprinted with yellow, red, and blue poppy flowers that swirled around green leaves and vines that looked wrinkled from being grabbed by rough hands. The dress met just above her thighs, and he could see that the red stockings had been ripped at the dress's hem. The thick white collar that hung over the neckline of the dress and the white sleeve cuffs were stained with black eyeliner and dried blood from wiping her eyes and face.

The slow trickle of tears began to stream down her cheeks heavier as her eyes met his dark brown gaze, flowing clear liquid and small flecks of black eyeliner into the corners of her mouth, rewetting the dried split of her busted lip. Richard's knees buckled under his weight at the sight of her. His hand extended towards the bottom of her chin, hoping to lift it just a little to assess how bad the damage was to her face, when Sophia flinched, her body stiffened and shrunk in fear. She was in shock and when he drew back, she almost immediately relaxed in the chair, the quivers vibrating through her were visible as if she was having a seizure. He attempted again and this time she was okay when she felt him taking her hand into his.

"Can you walk?" Richard's voice was baritone deep and unwavering. Inside, he was screaming as the veins in his neck and forehead pulsed into panic mode, but he knew that he couldn't show it. He had to be strong for her. Sophia shook her head in a dazed negative response. Her arms felt almost lifeless when he wrapped them around his neck to lift her out of the car. Her nose ran as her sobs increased, a mixture of tears and snot soaked the chest of his coveralls to the white undershirt beneath. He didn't care as long as she was safe.

His focus was on finding out what happened to her and who he had to possibly kill for hurting her. With a hard tap of his boot, he closed the Cadillac door causing him to swing Sophia towards the back passenger door. He caught a glimpse of the shiny brown leather suitcases piled up against the back seat before heading inside the open garage.

It wasn't until he got her under the florescent lights in the back room that he noticed the purplish-blue bruises on her thin neck and chin. Blotches of yellowish blue were forming at the corner of her lip around the split and up both sides of her thighs. He grabbed a bag of ice from the Frigidaire. The refrigerator door softly closed behind him as he walked over gently placing the bag against her lip. She winced at the coolness against the hot throbbing pain. He stood up calmly pacing the lime-colored concrete floor in front of her, his arms were risen above his head, fingers interlocked in a tight grip against his hair.

In mid stride he stopped pacing, his eyes were now matching hers in tears and reddish hue. Richard was burning hotter than a blue flame, but he never was the type to yell or lose his temper when upset. He kneeled in front of her, his eyes glancing at the large holes in the stockings, then back up into her eyes. "I'll kill him. For you Sophy, I'll kill him." were the only words he uttered before standing up and heading back to the garage to close the shop.

Part II: Sophia - Who Knew a Diamond Could Be So Heavy?

This diary belongs to:

Sophia Berte - De Luca

_____

Summer of 1959

San Jose, California

Saint Christopher Church

Diary,

I keep staring down at the empty space on my ring finger knowing that soon a diamond ring will be placed upon my bare skin. The stained arched glass depicting St. Christopher holding the Child Jesus is in the back room of Saint Christopher Church, the warm yellow sunlight shining through made their halos shimmer hues of gold and red. Shadows from a bird flying pass the windows appeared at the bottom of my simple white laced wedding dress. I wondered if I would go to Hell for thinking about another man instead of my betrothed on my wedding day. Then again between the combination of both Leo and my family there's about 100 people who are directly tied to the Mafia currently sitting in the church pews awaiting this event. Only God knows what some of them have done, and I think my infraction would seem minor in comparison to the eyes of the Lord.

When I first met Richard Hobbes, it was the Summer of 1955. We were teenagers, he was 19 years old, and I was 17 years old. I had gone with my father to an autobody shop downtown to get the headlight replaced on his Cadillac. I sat in the car while my father spoke with Mr. Lambert, the owner of the shop. My father took a pack of

Marlboro cigarettes out of his shirt pocket, lit one, and blew the smoke in Mr. Lambert's face. I could tell Mr. Lambert was displeased with the gesture, but too uncomfortable to say anything, maybe even too scared to move. Whenever I was with my father and saw him conducting the "family business" I never wanted to be in earshot of the conversation. Sometimes it was best to not know what was going on. That unawareness would come to bite me in the rear later. My father was purely Italian and looked every bit of it, very tall and round. His hair was thinning a little in the front, but he always kept it slicked back. He had green eyes too, that's where I got them from. My father was kind to our family, but scary to everyone else he knew and anyone looking right now could see the fear on Mr. Lambert's pale face as he passed my father some bills.

To the left of our Caddy stood a brown skinned boy of about 6'2 underneath an open garage door. He stared at my father as I stared at him. I had never seen a more handsome boy in my life, and I couldn't contain the flush of heat that arose in my cheeks when he finally noticed me in the passenger seat of the car. He smiled at me, and my father noticed. My father walked up to him, his face becoming redder in anger with each step. When he reached him, Richard was already backing up. My father knocked him to the ground with a hard fist to the chest. I could barely make out what he said but I'm sure he uttered a few nasty words and racial slurs at him. My eyes welled up with tears as I looked down at the floor of the car, embarrassed at what occurred. He stood over him waving his finger at him and then pointing towards me in the car, then he walked back to the car in a huff. He rounded the front and opened the driver's door slamming it shut furiously as Richard picked himself up. Richard retreated to the back of the garage with Mr. Lambert while another Italian man came rushing out of the garage to fix my father's headlight and once it was done, we headed back home.

I couldn't shake the feeling I had from Richard. He was in my thoughts every morning and in my dreams every night. One day I was on the way back home from a show and passed by the autobody shop. As I drove past the shop, I saw

Richard stepping out of a car he had moved to make way for another vehicle to enter the garage. There was nothing wrong with my car, but as I pulled into the body shop's driveway I decided that I had started hearing a funny noise coming from under the hood. I didn't know if he remembered me or if he hated me for what my father did to him, but when our eyes met I could tell we both felt the warm static feeling you get when you finally meet your soulmate.

Mr. Lambert stared at us from the garage door, smiling and shaking his head. I think he knew this day would come; it was just a matter of when it was going to happen. Richard towered over my slim 5'7 stature as I stood next to him under the opened hood. He looked around for a few minutes, adjusted some wires, and told me that the wires may have been the cause of the noise. We both knew that wasn't the case and I was full of it, but he never called me out on it. Mr. Lambert disappeared into the back while Richard was closing the hood.

When I offered to pay him, he waved his hand and said it was free of charge. He smiled at me lovingly and I melted inside. He then said in his confident tone that if I was free some evening, he would like to cook me supper. He remembered the trouble that my father caused and because of his status it would be better to have dinner at a private place. We chatted a few more minutes about our plans and I agreed to meet him at the shop for an early supper on Wednesdays since he worked the afternoon to evening shifts alone. I nearly jumped out of my skin saying yes as I rounded the car to the driver's side door. For the next 2 years we met in secret at the shop, enjoying each other's company and trying new foods together. On my 18th birthday we decided to take our relationship a little further. We both were virgins at the time and agreed that we would save ourselves for marriage, but that didn't mean we couldn't try other things.

Richard was the first and only man to bring me to orgasm with his mouth alone. I remember fondly the nights in the back of his old gray pickup truck. The rocking of the cab and squeaking of the bolts and coils as I climaxed with exalting power.

--Sophy

Part III: Two Demons in A Room Sipping Lemonade

Fall of 1959

San Jose, California

Manor of De Luca

Diary,

On my 21st birthday, my father came to my bedroom one morning saying he had the most amazing news to tell me. I smiled at him half-awake with my one eye opened, the other eye was squinting against the sunlight coming through the large windows. Up until this point I had a wonderful relationship with my father. I didn't know that it would change so quickly. My brown hair was shoulder length. I had set in pink curlers overnight and the hair that surrounded them was frizzed all over my pillows. He told me to get "all dolled up" and come downstairs he had someone for me to meet. I removed my curlers, letting the soft curls frame my face and placed the back of my hair in a high ponytail. I wore a yellow 3/4 sleeved dress that buttoned down the front that stopped below my knees with, white lace gloves, pantyhose, and matching colored heels. I stopped at the top of the steps hearing two male voices coming from the living room. It was my father's and another voice that wasn't familiar. When I reached the bottom step and peered into the room, I saw my mother holding a tray with a pitcher of lemonade four glasses filled with ice. My father and the mystery man now soon to be my husband was reaching for their individual glasses.

"Sophy! This is Leonardo De Luca. His father is in the business, and I want you two to get to know each other better." He was overjoyed at the financial gains.

Leo was 31 years old, short, and Italian. He stood up placing the glass on the coaster and clumsily adjusted the wrinkles out of his pants. He extended his hand to meet mine. I could see the clammy beads of sweat within his palm. I briefly placed my white gloved hand in his and quickly shook it. Little did I know that the hand shake I just did was the sealing of the deal between the Berte & the De Luca families. Who knew a diamond could feel so heavy? I can't help but tear up every few hours. It wasn't just coming to terms with the fact that the man I loved I could never be with or that I was marrying a pudgy fool like Leo, but the fact that my father who I loved and trusted sold me off to the puny bastard and his cruel family as earth shattering.

After the reception we arrived at a white stone mansion with a circular driveway and marble pillars - the Manor of De Luca. It was a beautiful home with green topiaries and flowers all around. The servants who opened the car door, taken my luggage, and gave me a tour of the house occasionally saw me crying. They smiled thinking it was just a nervous bride's tears of joy, but that couldn't be further from the truth. I wanted to scream that they were tears of regret, disgust, and total unhappiness, but the words couldn't escape my lips.

--Sophy

Part IV: Sophia - He's Ugly & He's A Cheater

Fall of 1960

San Jose, California

Emerald Isle Spa on Beverly Park

Diary,

Leo is a lying cheating fucking pig. The last time
he saw me naked is the last time he would ever
see me naked; you can bet on that! That is the
entry.

--Sophy

Winter of 1960

San Jose, California

Manor of De Luca

Diary,

I stare out this window surrounded by such a
beautiful prison, and the man who signed me up

for it has passed away. I would say I'm numb with emotion. The last couple of years of our relationship had been a turbulent one so you can imagine my surprise when I found out that I inherited $300,000 from my father's demise. Mother and father had divorced in 1959. He left her for his girlfriend named Sharon, who happens to be the same age as me. Mom was hurt for a while, but then realized it was better for her in the long run. She's been seeing her boyfriend since she got over it, started working out, and spends most of her time at the summer home in Italy. I love seeing her thrive. I long for that experience myself. But now that I have the money... wait... I think there's a noise coming from under the hood of my car. I hope I'm not too late.

--Sophy

Part V: Sophia - I Need a Tune Up

Winter of 1961 - New Year

San Jose, California

Manor of De Luca

Diary,

By the time I finished my errands it was 7pm. I
hoped that Richard's schedule was still the same
and that no one would be at the shop since it was
Wednesday. I drove to the shop and pulled into
the driveway, not knowing what I would say if he
no longer worked there, but to my surprise there
he stood in the same spot he has always stood in.
I practically leaped from the car into his arms. I
didn't know what his status was relationship wise,
and I didn't care. He closed the shop early that
night. We stood talking for hours in the side alley
next to the shop. The longer we talked the more
I needed to feel his touch. Although I had known
him all this time, he made me feel like the little
shy girl I was when I first saw him. He could tell
and with that he drew me close to him. My head
rested on the firmness of his chest. I huddled
inside his long navy overcoat, my arms wrapped
around the warmth of his waist. His heart paced
a steady rhythm under his button down. It

calmed me, being with him always calmed me. I breathed in the Spring night air. The spice of his cologne intertwined with its coolness. He squeezed me tight wrapping me in the folds of his coat. I purred at his grip and knew that for tonight I would be his.

He stared into my eyes as he placed the first of many kisses on my nose and lips. Our kiss was passionate and intense, too intense to be done outside. We broke away panting our warm breaths creating small, steamed clouds in front of our faces. He turned around and unlocked the side door to the shop and grabbed my hand, leading me into the garage. It was dark, you could see the orange streetlight reflecting orange hues on all the metal within the garage. He took me to Mr. Lambert's office which had a small tatter couch in front of the desk where many nights Mr. Lambert would sleep off his drunkenness away from Mrs. Lambert. We were both excited about the thrill of doing something mischievous in a place we shouldn't have been doing it. I knew we loved each other but this wasn't about love, it was about need. I needed him and he needed me. He bent me over the arm of the couch. My face inhaled the stale smell of the seat, it's smell of musk cologne and car parts.

I felt him pull down my panties and pantyhose, the cool air met my wetness sending a pleasurable jolt through my body. His pants fell to the floor, and I could hear him moan as he stroked himself. When we dated, we never had sex, only foreplay in those two years. So, my very first was unfortunately Leo. Leo was small, hairy, and I felt crushed under his weight. I had never experience anything remotely close to how I felt when Richard placed the tip of his penis at the entrance to my tight hole. He was gentle as he slid inside me, making sure it didn't hurt. He pumped deep and slowly, pulling out to the tip, then back deep inside.

I felt like a wild animal, moaning and thrashing all over the couch with every wave of orgasm. The pleasure was almost unbearable. He teased me with slow thrusts for what seemed like forever before he sped up. I realize now that he was making love to me. There was no space or time that would discourage him from making me feel good, even if that space was his boss's office on a beat-up couch. The blue light of morning shined through the dirty shop windows when we both finally felt filled, sated, and dropped in exhaustion. We knew then that the day had come when I would need to leave Leo. There was no way I could continue with Richard having him playing second fiddle to that ogre. And although I didn't think of it at the time, with how often we began making love, there was almost no way I was not going to get pregnant.

The morning after when I came home from my first evening with Richard, Leo wasn't home either. I assumed that he had overslept at one of his sleazy girlfriend's houses which I was okay with once I found out he was cheating on me. I took a long bath and climbed into bed, wishing that I never had to come back to this place, wishing I could find a way to leave. I didn't think that I was so lucky to get pregnant on our first time, but within the next couple of weeks I realized I couldn't catch my breath going up the stairs and every morning I felt a sicken urge to throw up whenever the servants made toast.

When the symptoms became unbearable, I made a doctor's appointment and went in for some tests. Leo and I had not had sex in years at this point, so I immediately knew when I received the positive pregnancy results that it was Richard's baby.

I was terrified. I didn't know what I was going to do. I hid the secret for a month before I told Richard. From that point on he did all he could for me in the hours I could be away from Leo. Richard was firm in wanting me to leave him now that I was pregnant. He was making great wages at Lambert's, and I always knew he wanted a family. A few weeks later I was secretly packed and planning my first attempt at leaving. I didn't know how dark life was about to become. On the morning that I was about to leave Leo, I walked into the dining room where he sat at the end of the table drinking coffee and reading the newspaper. The servants were laying out the last of the full breakfast feast on the table.

"What's all this for, Leo? Is there a party I wasn't aware of?" I asked hesitantly.

"No, doll. It's for you, come sit down." he said impatiently, not even looking up from his newspaper.

He was never a nice guy, and I was completely confused by his welcoming gesture. I should have realized that this was a warning. I sat down at the other end of the table, and he poured me a glass of orange juice from a beautiful small white glass pitcher. It had yellow and red poppies that contrasted against the white. I'll never forget that pitcher. I drank orange juice, had two slices of bacon, and 2 pancakes. After a while my stomach began to feel upset. I excused myself from the table and went upstairs to lay down. On my way through the kitchen, I picked up the telephone receiver to call Richard and once I felt Leo wasn't in earshot, I let him know that I would be late this evening and that I wasn't feeling well.

"Is everything alright with the baby?" He said concerned.

"Yes, I believe so. I think I just ate something that doesn't agree with us."

I hung up quickly and went upstairs, climbed back into bed and drifted off to sleep.

When I awoke the next morning, nauseated from oversleeping, but also doubled over in abdominal pain. I threw the comforter back and stood up. My legs felt weak and wobbly as I walked towards the bathroom. I looked in the mirror and found myself drenched in blood from the waist down. I screamed in terrified agony and two of our servants ran into the bathroom. I was rushed to the emergency room where I found out I had a miscarriage. I didn't get to speak to Richard for about two weeks as I lay in the hospital bed, recovering from the physical and emotional trauma. I didn't know how to tell him.

On the morning that I was released from the hospital I found out what truly happened. The taxi brought me home instead of Leo picking me up, which I welcomed. I walked past him deliberately ignoring his presence as I was too exhausted to have any kind of argument with him today. I went upstairs to our bedroom and began taking off my clothes for a bath.

I went into the bathroom releasing the plug to stop up the tub and turned the handle to the words "hot water". The hot water steamed up the mirrors in the bathroom and once I was submerged, I began to cry heavy tears into the soap's bubbles and suds. I knew at that point it was time to leave Leo before I had even found out there was a more devastating reason to leave.

After washing I dried myself off and threw on my favorite poppy dress. Its yellow, red, and blue flowers always made me smile. In my 20s I really got into the culture of the 60s style and loved thigh high dresses with colorful pantyhose. Today I wanted to be pretty, so I threw on my red pantyhose and placed my hair in a high bun. I applied thick black eyeliner to my eyes to make the green really pop. Once I was finished, I took a moment to admire myself. In all this time I had been focused on everything else but myself. I didn't notice when the bathroom door slowly opened. It was Leo and his face was bright red, his eyes were furious. I thought his head would pop off his shoulders.

Within seconds Leo's pudgy fingers were wrapped around my neck, his body towering over me as he screamed.

"You thought I wouldn't find out, did you? You fucking whore."

My hands were prying and clawing at his hands, arms, and chest. I was losing oxygen and losing it fast. The room was starting to spin as I gasped fewer breaths with each swing of my arms. He dropped me onto the floor, and I fell into a fetal position gasping raspy gulps of as much air as I could.

"You know how I found out! Your doctor called to check in two weeks ago and the bastard congratulated me on being a new father. WE haven't had sex in YEARS, SOPHIA! But don't worry! I fixed you up, but good! I fixed you up,

you whore and now there is no baby is there?"
his words stung, and spittle flew from his mouth
with every "x or th" sounding word.

His words hit me like a steam roller. He put
something in the orange juice to make me have a
miscarriage. I lost the baby because of him...

The anger boiled up inside of me and from waist
level I lunged all my body weight into his mid-
section knocking most of the wind out of him.
He reached back grabbing a handful of my hair,
punching me in the eye and head repeatedly. I
could taste the blood when he punched me in the
lip. I was still on my knees, my pantyhose ripping
across my thighs as I lunged and kicked at him.
The last thing I remember before going into total
shock was grabbing a fist full of the crotch of his
pants. I squeezed and twisted until he let go of
my hair. He now had fell to his knees and we
both were staring at each other bloody, swollen,
and scratched. I felt on the sink for a heavy
object and the first thing that I reached was the
soap dispenser. While I let his crotch go I
smashed the soap dispenser into the side of his

head. He rolled onto the ground and lay there unconscious. That was the day I knew that I had married Satan.

There was no time to waste. I packed as many suitcases as I could fill with all my stuff and demanded the servants to place them in my Cadillac. They had no objections after seeing my battered face. It was getting late now, and I only knew of one place to go and only one person I wanted to be with. I ran to the driver door of my car, started the engine, and peeled out of the driveway, gravel kicking up behind my wheels. I thought to myself it's now or never, Richard... now or never.

--Sophy

———————————

Part VI: Richard - Now or Never

"Sophy, I hear you but…"

"Richard!" Sophia had finally gained her ability to speak after the shock. "I have a little over $300,000 in a personal bank account from when my father passed away. I have everything I need to leave him now. I just need you, please, please say you'll go with me. We have so much time to have the life we wanted, together."

Richard knew what his answer would be. He loved her, he had waited for her.

Richard was never quite right after the loss of the baby. He never knew the full details, but his gut feeling told him that Leo had something to do with it. He knew that Sophia would never admit to that just to save him from going to jail for murder, but he knew, just like he knew one day he would even the score with him for hurting her or simply because he was just a miserable person. One way or another he was going to kill Leonardo De Luca as promised. Richard had his own savings stashed away for a rainy day or a brand-new baby room in his bi-level home off Sycamore Street. About a month ago, Mr. Lambert, who was well in his 80s passed away in his sleep. He didn't have any children, so he left the autobody shop to his longest and most loyal employee, Richard Hobbes. Richard was able to finally live comfortably, well as comfortable as a black man could be in America. He had no ties to California besides Sophia and wouldn't mind selling the shop. He took her hands in his once more and decided to leave with her. He just needed to plan for the inevitable which was Leo finding them. He knew Leo, and how corrupt he was and how he would never let her leave, so he needed to make sure he was ready for him for when that time came.

"We need to stop at my house for a few things and you need to get cleaned up. Then we can head to the airport." Richard kissed her forehead and held her hand as they walked out to the parking lot.

Part VII: Sophia - A Promise Well Kept

This diary belongs to:

Mrs. Sophia Hobbes

Summer of 1963

Maui, Hawaii

The Hobbes Bungalow

Diary,

I suppose the apple doesn't fall far from the tree in a family of crime. I may have been able to change my last name through a family connection back to my surname so that I would be able to marry Rich on the beautiful beach of Maui. That night in 1960 when we were fleeing California from Leo, we stopped at Rich's home to gather all his belongings. I took a shower in his bathroom removing the blood and dirt from my skin and hair. Then I grabbed a blue dress from my suitcase, redid my makeup, and was ready to begin our journey. Rich followed me in his pickup, and we dropped my Cadillac off at the parking lot of a nearby Ralphs. I left the keys in the glove compartment hoping a bum would steal it. We didn't want it anywhere near his house so he wouldn't be suspected of anything.

After we escaped from California, we traveled to the island of Hawaii, hoping to muddle any tracks that could be followed by Leo. I was hoping that he had died of a broken heart already, but I know he's too evil for that. Rich sold Lambert's Auto Body Shop for $30,000 giving us the down payment of our future home.

He and I settled in Hawaii, first we stayed at the Ritz Carlton in Room 415 for six months while house shopping until we found and bought a spacious bungalow with an oceanfront view. We took time christening each room at least twice, and a month later I threw up at the smell of Rich making toast. Now I'm 5 months pregnant and Rich has been wonderful at taking care of me and all my symptoms. I miss nothing of my old life except for my mother. I speak to her once a week, but I make sure not to tell her my location. Not because I think she would tell Leo, but because I wouldn't want it forced out of her at any point. She knows how Italian men can be. The night waves roll in softly against the golden sand. I watch the moonlight ripple across the tide as Richard rises from his chair to go get some more lemonade. His white linens blow in the warm air as he passes me by. I've never felt more at peace that I do right now, and I hope that it lasts for.......

A glass hits the tiled floor in the kitchen spraying shards in front of the stove and sink. Sophia hoists herself up from the hammock chair and waddles inside the opened glass sliding door. Her first sight is a medium size pool of blood trailing from the kitchen to the steps that lead to the bedroom levels. "Richard!" She calls up the stairs, her own voice frightening her. She hears thuds and rumbles across the floor and then gunshots. She races up the stairs skipping a step or two but also trying to be mindful that she's carrying an extra load. She heads down the long hallway to the bedroom at the end, the door is slightly ajar. She pushes the door slowly opening it up to view the end of their king size bed. The beige carpet is smeared with copious amounts of blood. She slowly crept into the room holding her stomach, bracing herself for what could come next. She rounds the corner; her eyes stretch wide and the olive tone in her face melts to a pale ivory. Laying on the bed clutching his chest is Leo. Their cream-colored sheets are pooling with blood, whatever weapon he may have had was gone.

Leo's eyes were staring up at the ceiling as she appeared next to him. They slowly rolled to the side to stare at her face and as their eyes met, his eyes went still. "Richard!"! Richard! Please! Where are you?!" she yelled, opening the closet doors and checking the balcony. She ran to the landline and called the police and an ambulance then she noticed the bloody handprint on the bathroom door. She ran as fast as she could over to the door and pushed it open. On the sink was a 6-inch blade covered in blood. The blood trailed to the bathtub where the shower curtain was closed but still waving gently. She was terrified at what she might see next. She held her stomach as she pulled the curtain back.

"Sophia, my child, I can't tell you that I know your pain. There are no excuses for that night. I hated him for what he had done." Mia said.

"I could never undo what happened, but I saved you for you to get your revenge."

"REVENGE ON WHO?! You fed from Richard, and he fed from my child AND me. A part of me can never forgive you for that."

"On us both if you'd like."

"You're a killer. We are killers. That's how we live. He was DEAD WRONG though and needs to pay." Emily exploded. She hated him so much.

"Emily." Mia reached to calm her.

"NO!"

"See I didn't want to do this, but I owed you both an explanation."

SIX

THE STALKING GROUNDS

Spring 1955 - Harlem, New York

Mia sat at a table in the Lenox Lounge on 125th street listening to Miles Davis blow. The chair across from the little square table from her was empty while she waited for Emily to arrive. Miles smelled delicious, she glamoured the whole room just to get a taste of his talent. His heartbeat was so calm as he played refrain and riff on his trumpet. She didn't notice when he sat down at her table.

"Have I seen you somewhere? Maybe in a Paris Museum full of great Moorish busts and statues." Michael fingertips glided across Mia's shoulder.

Michael was 6'1 his black trench coat was draped over the back of the chair. He wore a navy-blue suit, a white dress shirt, and a matching navy-blue tie. His eyes were a deep shade of brown with a light hazel tint in the middle, like warmed milk in coffee.

"Did you just use the word "Moorish" in 1955? That's definitely a red flag for racism." Mia pretended to wipe where he touched with the napkin she held under her drink.

"I've been watching you all evening."

"All these women, booze, and dancing around and you've been focused on me, what was the point of even coming here?" She laughed at him. It was a beautiful laugh but he hated that she found him a fool.

"Well, I was passing by, looking for something to eat, and was drawn to you."

"A white man in Harlem at a predominately Black dance hall? I see. You are racist, aren't you? Coming to the Black neighbors for your hunt."

"Ha no, in fact..." he ran his fingers through his short deep brown hair. "...I'm the most Liberal of all of my friends and quite the feminist."

"Wow you have friends... that's hard to believe. Well dear, I won't be one of them so go away." Mia stood up and walked away from Michael grabbing a sit at the bar.

Instantly Michael was sitting in the sit next to her at the bar.

"Are you going to make getting to know you a challenge? Because if so I'm up for it."

"So, you're one of those people that need a challenge to be won. I see. Listen, I rather not know you. Right now, I don't even like you." Mia lit a cigarette and flicked it at him. She wasn't even a smoker. She just wanted him to leave.

"But you're the only one like me here… wait."

They both smelled a familiar aroma of fresh blood walk into the door. They turned towards the entrance to see Emily checking her coat at the coat check window.

"And then there were three of us. She's family, fuck with her and that's fucking with me and from what I can tell I'm much older than you so don't test me."

"Ohh the mouth on you. As you wish, doll, but I will woo you by the end of the night. You just watch and see." He stood up from the bar, placing his hands in the pockets of his suit pants and made an overly confident stride over to a corner table in front of the band. He waived the waiter over and ordered a drink we both knew he would not drink.

Mia ordered Cognac and pretended to drink it. She liked the taste of brandy but knew she couldn't swallow it without getting deathly sick and with a creature like him on the prowl she knew she had to be sharp just in case. She surveyed the room taking one more glance at Mr. Ego and then walked over to Emily.

"Pet or Prey?" Emily asked with a humorous tone.

"Neither...?" Mia scoffed.

"Really? she prodded. "Hey, what is it with you tonight?"

"I don't know. I guess I'm just trying to distract myself." Mia looked around the room and met eyes with Michael again this time he was at another table in line view of where she was standing.

Without speaking Mia's words were clear and directly in the mind of Emily. "The navy suit is a vampire too. I don't trust him."

"Geez did he come up to you? What did you say to him?" Emily questioned.

"I said go away, ghoul."

"But why maybe he's a match I mean he's handsome."

"Not likely."

"Hey ladies, you know I have that gift too, most of US do." Michael saluted Mia and Emily with a grin from across the room.

"See, a fucking ghoul."

"Michael, that's my name. Michael Harrington. Mr. Harrington if you want, but never ghoul." he chimed in.

"Are you going to make me beg? Because if you're into that you know I can make it happen."

"Beg then, fucking ghoul." Mia got her coat and walked out of the entrance.

And he did beg, every single night for the next 7 years, and Mia loved it.

SEVEN

TURN, BABY, TURN

Summer 1963 - Maui, Hawaii

Mia's legs straddled Richard's waist from behind as he laid bleeding out in the bathtub. She was so distracted by the thirst that she hadn't even heard Sophia open the bathroom door. It wasn't until the thud of Sophia passing out on the tile that Mia lifted her head from Richard's neck.

The vibrant brown of her eyes was rimmed with red as she stared at the pregnant woman on the floor. She could hear both of their hearts beating in the silence of the room.

In a blur of speed Michael stood above Sophia's motionless body. His nails grew long and sharp like box cutters on a huge bat like hands although the rest of his had still been his human form. Mia's thoughts strayed to her mother laying lifeless on the Moroccan dirt. The white men standing around her grinning and shouting at her lifeless corpse. Sophia's face blended with her mother's as she became aware of what Michael was about to do. She couldn't move from the shock and with his big, fanged grin Michael sliced Sophia's lower abdomen open with one swipe. Blood splashed all over the cabinets and tile. Sophia shot up in a sitting position on the floor letting out a blood curdling scream before passing out again; the same final noise that Mia's mother had made. Michael reached in, dark red blood pooled underneath her as he grabbed the still forming baby from Sophia's stomach and sunk his teeth into the baby's skull. Michael smiled at Mia and said slyly, "Two for one!"

Mia let out a was horrified at his barbarism. Bloody tears ran down her face as she leaped from Richard and onto Michael's back with all her strength. The fetus fell to the floor with a wet plop that Mia would never forget. She sunk her claws into this neck tearing at his flesh, scratching his face, and damaging one eye. Michael was caught off guard and tried everything to shake her off. He threw Mia into the mirror above the sink, shared fell onto the floor and Sophia. Once free he jumped out of the window, they had initially come in and vanished.

Mia rolled off the sink and landed on the floor next to Sophia in the fetal position. She was met face to face with the concaved head of the fetus when she let out a beastly scream, one that startled Michael even at the distance he had run. Mia lay there looking at all the blood. Hating herself for being a monster. She sat up and crawled over to Sophia placing her head on her lap. A faint heartbeat lingered in her body and through screaming bloody tears Mia bit a gash into the inside of her forearm. The wound bubbled with blood, and she pressed it to Sophia's mouth.

"You'll get your revenge just like we did."

"Soph, I don't have a blood pact with him, but a soul bond maybe. I knew him… I knew him before I met him in '55. It was just a feeling I got like a whisper into the ether. He was everything I was and wanted to be. He was my weakness. We were monsters, ARE monsters and after you and your family… I didn't know how horrific he could be, how horrific I was. I vowed to never see him again that night and disgraced I ran in '64 leaving you with Em. For everything I am sorry."

EIGHT

———

LUCKY'S LAUNDROMAT

Summer 2002 - Thermal, California

It's mid-day, Candace adjusts her sunglasses against the bright high noon sunshine as she slows down her light blue 1989 Oldsmobile Calais at the stop sign of Cricket Lane. She places her strawberry blonde curls into a high ponytail that reaches her shoulders. She's always had long thick curly blonde hair, and every time she attempted to straighten it the hot California heat always reverted it back to her natural state. Her left turn signal clicks slowly as she pulls onto Route 111 headed towards Thermal, white desert sand kicking up creating dusty swirls behind her wheels. She sighs at the thought of finally being able to do the mountain of laundry that she had put off for the past week while studying for finals. It was the last chore to do on a very long list of chores.

Candace rolls down her window letting the hot breeze blow little wisps of hair to frame around her face. She steps on the gas and the red line on the speedometer pushes to 75. The road is long, but the journey is short. She arrives at a dusty laundromat. A sign hangs above the sandstone building in bold yellow and orange font, Lucky's Laundromat. Next door to Lucky's is an old Texaco gas station.

A young man in a red and white Texaco shirt stands behind the counter. He was grinning from ear to ear looking down at his phone completely distracted. Candace hated that about young people. She thought that it made them all look bad when one was caught on their phone while they were working. She was 25 years old but still included herself in the "young people" group. She looked around at the deserted gas pumps and thought to herself "It's a small gas station in a big desert and people rarely come out this far unless they're tourists, not a big deal."

She sits there staring through her windshield into the laundromat's big glass windows. The heat off of the navy-blue leather seats begins to sting her legs and butt just below the cut off of her blue jean shorts. The laundromat was empty, and the lights were off, but there was a big orange sign saying **WE'RE OPEN** taped to the glass door letting her know she could go inside. She stepped out of the car leaving the windows open and slamming the door shut. The door lock makes a loud clicking noise when she presses the circular metal plunger down to lock the driver door. Her sneakers kick up dirt and gravel as she heads toward the trunk of the car. The keys jingle in her hand when she opens the trunk. She grabs the three red, white, and blue laundry bags and detergent out of the back. A bus kicks up dust and dirt as it rides down the baren road. She looks at the back of the bus and the torn ad shows Joe the Camel with a logo in bright red that reads "I'd Walk a Mile for a Camel". She leered at the idea of smoking and continued scraping along the old, cracked asphalt towards Lucky's.

Candace grabs the aluminum door handle and pulls open the door to walk inside the laundromat. The lights turned on automatically emitting a warm yellow light from the fluorescent bulbs in the ceiling. She stood at the door taking the room in. She had been here before, but never noticed its details. It was a medium sized four cornered room with yellow and blue flowered wallpaper, white tile with dried water stains here and there, and fifteen shiny silver laundry machines.

In one of the corners was a small hallway that led to a unisex bathroom. She expected the AC to be at full blast but was greeted by even more heat than what she felt outside. The sweat began to bead on her forehead, neck, and under her medium sized tits almost immediately. As she placed the first load of laundry in the washer, droplets of sweat rolled down her stomach forming two small imprints on the outside of her white tank top. The shorts and the tank top were all she had clean to wear. She looked down at her outfit and shrugged, "it was too hot for normal clothes anyways."

After an hour her clothes were soaked with sweat. She reached above the washing machine adding detergent to her next load. You could just make out the perky rounded shape of her deep rose-colored nipples through her almost see through tank top. She placed the detergent on a chair next to a laundry cart. On the wheel of the cart stuck a white piece of paper with bold black marker writing:

LUCKY'S LAUNDROMAT!
ATTENTION PATRONS!
THE LAUNDROMAT AC IS BROKEN
AND WILL BE FIXED ON TUESDAY.
WE'RE SORRY FOR THE
INCONVENIENCE.

Today was Thursday so obviously it hadn't been fixed.

Beads of sweat ran down her back and in between her breasts. She wiped her face with the back of her hand as she sat on the white folding table across from the dryers. The metal legs rocked a little beneath her 5'9 frame. She glanced over at the only vending machine. A giant perspiring Sprite bottle was photographed on the outside. She yearned for a cool drink, anything with ice. Her eyes then landed on the white and red out of order sign at the bottom of the machine. She checked her pockets for extra change or her debit card so that she could get something from the gas station but realized she left home with only her driver's license. At that point she was SOL. "What a day this had turned out to be." She closed her eyes and sighed in disdain.

With her eyes closed she drifted away into a fantasy of fresh ice cubes gently glided down her neck. The cool melted droplets running between her breasts, down her stomach and pooling in the smooth indent of her belly button. Each nipple being encircled with ice and then kissed and sucked. Her nipples becoming firmer and firmer with each breath of cool air. Her hand caressed up her neck as her back tensed and arched at the sensation. She felt so good that she forgot about the heat, the laundromat, and the fact that she was in public. She didn't notice the glass door opened and the man who walked in.

Candace cooed softly at her own touch. Her fingertips worked their way down her neck, across her stomach, to the top of her shorts. She couldn't stop herself as her fingertips tapped a rhythm on the crotch of her shorts. She slid her hand between the tightness of the front of her shorts and her lower stomach reaching closer and closer to her pus...... Candace's eyes jolted opened to the sharp metallic dropping of coins from the coin machine. A tall bronze skinned man about 6'1, wearing a grey baseball cap, red t-shirt and dark Greyson sweatpants was bent over picking up the last of the quarters at the bottom of the tray. His blue duffel bag full of laundry and a bottle of Gain sat on the floor next to his foot. His beard was full of silky midnight black hair. He was older than Candace, about 35. His body screamed fantasy novel to her, and his sultry dark eyes were strong and mysterious.

Their eyes met and lingered for a minute too long. Realizing the too long pause Candace shuddered and shyly broke the gaze. There was no way he didn't see her caressing herself and moaning on the top of the folding table. She didn't exactly know how long he had been standing there. Candace's eyes were everywhere in the room besides looking at him. He looked at her as if he felt bad for interrupting her moment.

Embarrassed and extremely horny she quickly hopped off the table and went to the washing machine. She placed her wet clothes into the dryer, added her quarters and pressed START. She hurried as she nervously started another wash and then made a quick exit to the bathroom. She locked eyes with the mystery man one more time before closing the bathroom door.

The sweat on her shirt pressed into her back as she leaned against the chipped white painted door. Between the heat and her insatiable lust for a man's touch she couldn't be in the same room as him. Candace turned the faucet on and splashed cold water on her face. The coolness flushed over her warm eyes, nose, and lips sending her back into the fantasy with the ice. She placed her now cold hands around the back of her neck releasing a low moan. The buzzer on one of the dryers she occupied went off in the distance.

She took one last look in the mirror adjusting her clothes and smoothing her ponytail before unlocking the door and turning the knob. The door popped open with a thud and to her surprise the mystery man was standing outside the door. It was silent except for the whirring of the laundry machines. She could hear her heart pounding through her skin as she stared into his almond-shaped brown eyes. He opened his lips to speak, and a deep inquisitive tone emerged, "Can I help you in there?"

Without hesitation she grabbed the collar of his red T-shirt, pulled him into the bathroom and closed the door. Both of Candace's palms were placed on the door as she stared at the floor tiles in shock. She couldn't believe what she had just done. The door felt cooler now on her palms than it did on her back earlier. She grabbed the old golden doorknob and clicked the lock in.

It seemed like it took forever for her to turn around and face him, but when she did, he had already taken off his shirt. His arms, chest, and stomach sculpted beautifully. She took him all in, admiring the silky black hair on his arms, chest, and trailing down his stomach. Candace gripped the bottom of her tank top and raised it over her head in one quick motion. She began walking towards the mystery man, tits bouncing with every step. Her erect nipples pressed firmly onto his chest as she kissed him intensely, her hands searching for the drawstring on his sweatpants. She finds it and begins to untie the knot quickly. He stumbles into the corner of the room as she pushes him back, using the wall to stabilize himself and her weight.

She steps back second thinking the whole encounter and while staring into his eyes she whispers, "I don't even know your name." It's uh Javi... Her fingers rose quickly to his mouth. "Shh! never mind, I don't want to know. I want this to remain unnamed, a mystery, fun you know." Candace drops to her knees. The cold white tiles press into her skin. She drags his sweatpants and boxers slowly down as she goes. His dick was semi hard. She grasps its softness, slowly stroking back and forth.

He vibrated, yearning to feel the wetness of the back of her throat. His dick became harder as she stroked with one hand, her other stable on his opposite thigh. She gets close to the head marveling at how thick it is, a small coat of wetness on the tip. She looks up at him and he notices her large blue eyes have specks of emerald, green around the irises. He marveled at the beauty and innocence in her face. Her hair was wild with curls but tamed by one white scrunchie. He braced himself against the corner as she opened her mouth.

Candace's pink tongue jutted out of her mouth and began to lick the underside of his dick's head. He shuddered at the sensitivity. Her tongue circled around the tip a few times and then she took the whole head and shaft into her mouth. "Fuck!" he gasped, and she could feel his dick pulse in her mouth. She glided his dick out of her mouth in one long hard sucking motion, ending with an audible pop. Her cheeks sunken in on both sides of her face created a vacuum-like seal around his tip and a fish like appearance. She stroked his dick while taking him into her mouth a second time, then a third, and fourth. She was picking up speed and he was beginning to shake.

Candace was no expert on blowjobs and everything she learned she knew from watching porn. She decided to try a technique that she had seen one night while watching with an ex. She placed her hands on his bare hips, digging her nails into his sides. She took a deep breath and rammed his dick down her throat and that sent him over the edge. Tears streamed down her face as she made gagging noises and continued to deep throat him.

He was about to cum but was nowhere near ready to let it end this quickly. He bent down and kissed her hard on the lips, then he grabbed the base of her ponytail and began to wrap her hair around his hand.

He placed his other hand at the bottom of her jaw and opened her mouth as wide as it could go. His dick was throbbing, and he wanted all of her, he needed her. Her eyes stretched in surprise at his sudden change of pace and dominance, but she loved the roughness he was inflicting. It made him even more of a mystery in her eyes. He placed his thumb in her mouth and she sucked obediently. He moaned at the feeling of her soft wet tongue rolling around his coarse digit. He moved forward out of the corner causing her to fall onto her butt. He guided her to the wall by the hand that was gripping her hair and she was now sitting on the floor, her legs in between his as he stood above her with her back against the white wall.

He bent over one last time and whispered in her ear, "This is a perfect position for a throat fucking, baby girl." She smiled lustfully and he grabbed her hair tighter. Her perfect tits quickly rising and falling with every deep breath. He placed his hand against the wall holding her head still while he stroked his dick in front of her face. She smirked at him realizing in that moment that the roles of dominant and submissive had reversed. She had pulled him in the bathroom and now he was holding her by the hair. She looked in his eyes and with a sinister smile said, "Lucky's Laundromat, well today's been my lucky day." She opened her mouth sticking out her tongue to its full length mimicking her best impression of Hentai porn while inviting him to use her throat.

Candace hovered over the sink grabbing a handful of cool water to rinse out her mouth while Michael pulled up his sweatpants and put his shirt back on. She looked at him from the mirror and gave a mischievous smile over her shoulder.

"That was fun." she said while reaching for the bathroom doorknob. She went to turn it, but the door wouldn't budge.

"It sure was, Candace.... but I think the fun's just beginning."

"How did you know my name?"

She began to panic, pulling at the door as hard as she could. The lights began to flicker on and off in the bathroom. The light from under the door was the only constant light until everything went black. Candace fell against the toilet, feeling the tile on her legs once more. She was crying and sobbing wishing that the night was over.

"It will be over soon enough, Candace." A voice said from the dark.

Michael grabbed her hair and pulled her up to stand. He could feel her heartbeat quicken the same way it had when he touched her.

"It's funny how your heartbeat sounds the exact same as when your fucking, as when you're scared. I like that sound."
Michael laughed.

He licked the long of her neck tasting her sweat mixed with her tears.

"Say you like this."

"Say you want this."

"SAY IT, CANDACE!"

"I want this..." she murmured through tears. "Please don't hurt me."

"Okay... Okay. My sweet little angel." He whispered while cupping the sides of her face, his thumb swiping across the dried blood on her bottom lip. Her eyes closed for a moment hoping he would go away. When she opened her eyes, he had disappeared into the darkness.

His blood shot eyes watched her. He could hear her heartbeat thump in her chest. He listened to her cry and whimper, gathering the courage to stand up. She palmed the walls, feeling her way around the room towards the door. She was reaching out into the blackness for the doorknob when he flung himself at her with all his force, plunging his fangs deep into her neck. The tiles behind her back and head shattered into shards, piercing her skin, and falling to the ground in a spray. Candace screamed in pain, but her mouth was silenced by the force of his hand. She bit down into his palm and his blood poured into her mouth. He drank her into sweet obedient silence. Her cries became soft delusional whines as she faded into death.

Michael left the bathroom in the mess that it was. Candace's body wedged between the sink and what was left of the broken tile wall. He closed the bathroom door with little regard for the scene, leaving the clothes in the washer, they weren't his to begin with. The owner was dead outside the laundromat stuffed into the driver side cab of his red pick-up truck. The sun continued to blaze when Michael went outside. He made note of the security camera and walked to the other side of the building to a parked BMW.

His eyes burned from the sun, but nothing, a new pair of sunglasses which he took from Candace couldn't fix. At least for the time being.

Once he reached out of security view, his skin faded from bronze to beige, his hair once dark and curly was a dark brown prep boy school cut. He even had the ability to change his clothes at will from red T-shirt and gray sweatpants to a white polo shirt with beige chinos. He did a quick turn around and headed to Texaco, picked up a Mars bar, and headed back to the BMW. He threw the candy bar into the back seat and pulled out of the parking lot.

NINE

NEVERMORE

Fall 2022 - Los Angeles, California

Richard, my sweet Richard. Years had gone by since that night on the island. Now all that was left of Richard had become a pile of dusty memorabilia in a medium brown box that sat in the corner of the bungalow.

A box filled with the memories of happiness, memories that have been tormenting my every thought. The nights we spent in each other's arms were gone, and the nights alone wrapped in my bed sheets had reappeared.

I often wonder what happens to people like me, people who want love, but can't seem to keep it no matter how hard they hold on.

Do our hearts even beat the same when love is lost? Or do we gradually learn to cope with the emptiness and irregularity of its new rhythm? Is there anything to make us whole? Well, an eternity is a long time to figure the answers out.

Sophia sat on the piano bench, her back pressed against the coolness of the keys staring out into the night sky, her thoughts flying by slowly like the planes over the city. Mia sat next to her while Emily danced playfully around the drunken bartender in the kitchen.

"Did you ever find love again? After I left..." Mia placed her hand upon Sophia's hand resting on the bench.

"I locked myself in my apartment with books, art, and television when you left, wasting away the years. I was confused. Mourning and infuriated. Parts of me hated you, despised you, and still does... for what you took from me, what HE took from me, but I love you... as my sire and creator who brought me this gift. I spent a lot of time plotting revenge instead of knowing you and discovering the new me. So, around

2009 I started painting. One evening I was hunting in east LA, and I passed a gallery space. There I met...." she hesitated, deciding if she should trust her with the truth. "His name is Nick."

"Oh, so he's current. Is he one of us?"

"Something like that..."

Summer 2010 - East of Downtown Los Angeles, CA

Sophia applied her perfume to her neckline, giving herself the once over in the mirror. She didn't care for the New Age style of dress where everything was almost nude, but she didn't want to stand out with her 60s fashions. When Emily arrived, she was floored by the amount of cleavage Sophia was showing. Sophia was decked out in a black sleek spaghetti strapped satin dress; her dark hair was slicked back in a neat bun. The dark chestnut eye shadow made her green eyes bright like a feline and her lips were a soft matte burgundy.

"Sophie! You look breath taking!" Emily exclaimed as she stood in the open car door of the Uber.

"I just put a little number together, trying something new." She did a little dancing spin on the curbside.

Sophia looked down at her phone as they piled into the black Mercedes and were on their way to the art show.

The entrance of the art studio was brightly lit and welcoming. The stark white walls were a brilliant contrast to the colorful artwork and the red brick that separated them.

The girls partook in the arts whenever they were together. Both she and Emily haven't been out since Mia left. Sophia felt that her new self could fit in this space. She decided tonight that she would immerse herself in the arts, love passionately, and find a particular man she had her eye on for the last few weeks.

One painting by an artist named N. Richardson mesmerized her. The Richard in Richardson brought back a flood of memories of her mortal life, sneaking off together after dark.

On the canvas were beautiful spirals of neon blues, purples, pinks, and green. It had a feminine quality, but the spirals of navy blue made her think of the dangers lurking in the night. It fit her perfectly and she knew that she would have it hanging in her living room by the end of the night.

Nick stood aimlessly at the bar while his agent went on about his work to a potential buyer. He felt an urge, subtle, soft, but powerful. He gulped his whiskey double before turning around. Sophia stood fixated on his painting as he approached her. "You like that one?" a deep voice asked from behind her.

Sophia turned to meet Nick's gaze. He was the one she had been waiting for, but how did he know. His smiling face stood 6'2 to her 5'7 frame. He wore a black silk button down with a matte vest and black dress pants. His long dark dreads neatly fishtailed down his back in a French braid. He was quite dapper she thought as her eyes trailed down his body. She laughed when she noticed they were matching.

Her smile faded into a flush of heat in her cheeks, her last meal making her olive skin rosy, then he began to speak again.

"I feel like I've seen you before. Maybe in a dream." He was staring into her eyes. He didn't realize that he was touching her arms.

"I'm sorry, – Nick Richardson aka N. Richardson. And your name?"

"Sophia Hobbes." She extended her hand, her palm was warm, but her fingertips were like icicles. She noticed and so did he. She quickly drew back and changed the subject. "So, you created this piece? It is extremely expressive. What was your muse?"

"I painted that, after a dream. For the last few weeks before bed I've been feeling this feminine energy, it's radiant. I would lay awake at night thinking about it, so I decided to put it on canvas."

"It's kind of like you…"

"Me?" She jested.

"Yeah, you're radiant. You ooze femininity, power, and mystery from your skin, your smile. It's not a pickup line I swear, it's just the truth, and I'm observant." He tapped the side of his head.

Sophia didn't know what to say to that. She could feel her stomach tightening and nipples hardening under her dress. They were clearly visible now for all to see and she didn't care.

"Hey, I only have to be here another hour, you want to get out of here?"

"It's getting late, and I'm sure your girlfriend Mr. Richardson…"

""Mr. Richardson, I like the way you say it." he smiled. "And Girlfriend?" Nick asked with an upturned nose.

"Well, I just assumed, I mean you're young and look great."

"You're young too."

"Yeah right." Emily telepathically chimed in with a giggle. "Tell him about those original Wrangler bell bottoms you wore in the 70s."

"If it's safe to be forward I'd like to explore more of you... artistically, if you're willing? I do my best work at night." He leaned into her; his lip caresses her earlobe. "You've got an hour to decide, look around, drink some wine, get chill, and at the end of the night, be mine." He whispered gently. Nick stepped back and tapped her iPhone with his. His contact information appeared immediately on her screen. "Meet me at my place, before midnight." Sophia stared at his broad shoulders as he walked away to a potential buyer.

"That gives you roughly 6 hours until sunrise, go get em killer." Emily echoed in Sophia's mind which was returned by a snarky hit bump.

Sophia was hesitant to meet Nick at his place. There was something about him that she couldn't put her finger on. Perhaps that was what drew her to him from the beginning. He had a power about him too, prince worthy, something in his eyes, his hands, his stride was royal. The longer she thought about him as she gazed upon the whimsical paintings. She wasn't sure if she could control herself in his presence.

Her dark side was starting to rear its ugly little fangs and he smelled so good, in more of a perfectly seared steak way than a good Cologne way. Talented people were a rare find. Their gifts were embedded in their DNA and to a vampire it smelled delicious. That's why vampires are so attracted to the arts, the smell of creativity had a juiciness to it. And to drink of a gifted person was to acquire their gifts without any of their weaknesses. Drain a sculptor become a sculptress without arthritis and so on.

---

4 Weeks Earlier (1:00am) - East Downtown Los Angeles, CA

Sophia frequently hunted in East LA. "You never hunt in your own town." Mia's words re-played in her ears as she flew over the city. Not all vampires can fly, but she had enough time to learn that she had the ability while she was hiding from her feelings and the world.

One evening above the clouds Sophia felt a sudden euphoric sensation that distracted her long enough that she almost fell out of the sky. She tumbled freefalling through wispy clouds with no fear. She felt at peace, the same peace she felt when she was with Richard. She let go of the feeling just enough to catch herself before hitting the ground. The streetlights glowed a hard orange and the only soft light was coming from the top floor of a nearby loft. The euphoria from the loft carried her to a side window and there she sat on the fire escape watching a young man paint.

Sophia had been watching him for weeks now. At night after the hunt, she would sit on his fire escape watching him paint, soaking in his essence. His dark locs hanging down over his chiseled mocha bare chest. Seeing the smears of paint in between the pulsing veins of his strong hands while wiping them on an old painter's cloth. She wanted him. Badly.

The smell of his sweat on her skin. His heartbeat was pounding in her ears, stronger than most humans, almost like a snake's rattle in warning. He was painting a beautiful nude woman that in a way resembled her. He stood in front of the canvas, his arms crossed and hand stoking his beard, legs spread wide above the tarp taking in what he had created. He placed the paint brushes into the water filled mason jar and headed to the bathroom. A few minutes later Sophia could hear the shower running and then steam crept around the cracks of the bathroom door.

He came out with a towel wrapped around his waist and he sat on the end of his bed, grabbed his phone, and started going through text messages. He stood up dropping the towel from around his waist. Sophia's eyes widen as she looked at his long thick legs and supple ass. His dick was soft but even soft it looked about 6 inches long and thick. She licked her lips at the thought. He put on some boxers and a pair of basketball shorts and climbed into bed. When he turned the lights out Sophia backed away from the window. She was about to leave when she heard his heartbeat quicken. His hand moved steadily under his sheets as he stroked himself slowly. She watched him pleasure himself until climax.

That night when she got home, she played with herself. A long silver vibrator created a low hum in between her thighs. She paced her breathing, the vibrations deep in her pelvis, quaking under her skin. She needed him, needed to know him. Her hips strummed back and forth, the waves of her pulsing g-spot crashing against the toy edging her closer to eruption. All she could see was his eyes, a deep shade of brown that melted her soul when she exploded. "Mr. Richard...son."

2010 Summer - East of Downtown Los Angeles, CA

Sophia stood at the bar, caressing her own neck without thinking about it. She felt the sensation of her fingertips but did not attribute that to her own pleasure. She just knew that she was hot and could feel the dampness in her panties beginning to soak through. It was hard to be in the room with him without staring at his lips, seeing through those dress pants at the heavy tool she knew he carried. Her breathing was heavy, she could hear it with ever rise and fall of her chest.

"Pet or Prey, either way! You're going!" Emily was grinning from ear to ear as she gingerly sprinted up to the bar. "Do you know him!? He seems to know you." Emily's hip nudged her elbow.

She was still weighing her options, go home alone and do her normal routine or go out and experience something different. She had already fed for the night but being around him was making her hungry in more ways than one. She walked out of the gallery into the cool summer evening air. Emily met her at the curb.

"What are you doing, Em?"

"Waiting for the Uber I called for you."

"I'm walking "home" with that guy over there." She pointed at a young white guy whose intentions for her were more than just walking.

"You know I love the bad ones." Emily laughed.

When the Uber arrived, Sophia got in and headed home.

Sophia unlocked the door of her apartment. She took a quick shower and once out she rummaged through boxes of clothes in her closet. All of her clothes and lingerie were out of date. She looked at the clock its neon blue face reflecting 11:09pm. She pulled out a black baby doll dress that stopped right above the knees. She sat on the end of her bed second guessing herself as she looked at the light blue veins that ran through her olive ample breasts.

Maybe I should feed again just in case, she thought. Ugh blood breath though, gum can't even cure that. She applied her vanilla whipped body lotion to her skin, a few sprits of perfume to her thighs, and two dabs behind her ears. Sophia laid outstretched across her sheets staring at the ceiling letting the time tick away. She looked over at her phone on the night stand its black screen smudged with her fingerprints. She reached for it and the blue light shined bright against her face. Her fingers hovered over the glowing font of Nick's phone number as she hit the text message.

"Hi Nick, it's Sophia I'm leaving now. See you soon."

Three dots appeared beneath her message immediately after she hit send.

"See you soon, Sophia."

Sophia laid the phone on her chest and laughed like a schoolgirl. She allowed the phone screen to go back to black and rolled off her bed to leave.

The Uber drive wasn't long, but the anticipation was building as each green mile marker passed reflected in the headlights. She wasn't about to mess up her hair by flying to his apartment.

Being timed made her pussy vibrate in a way that it had never had with the vibrator or with any partner. That awakening feeling was happening again but this time she wasn't alone in her bed or shower. She was on high alert for all her senses. Her sense of smell was more prominent; blood thirst was stronger. She always appeared timider than the ladies in her circle, but a rage boiled inside her that could melt metal. Tonight, she felt animalistic, ravenous, and wild.

She arrived outside of his loft around 12:10am. She dialed his phone from her car.

"Hello beautiful, when you're inside get on the elevator and press 8. I'll be waiting for you at the door."

Her legs felt like Jell-O as she got out of the car and walked into the lobby. She watched the numbers on the dial above the elevator count down to the first floor. She felt the jitters welling up in her stomach as the elevator came to a stop on the 8th floor. The elevator binged and the doors opened. Sophia's satin reflected in the candlelight. Nick stood at the door shirtless and barefoot in casual linen pants.

Sophia felt slightly overdressed.

"I'm glad you decided to come." The smile he gave was mischievous.

"I'm glad you invited me."

Sophia walked into the penthouse and remained silent as she took in the landscape. This was the highest up she had ever been and seeing the city from this view was gorgeous. She fell in love with Los Angeles all over.

Nick grabbed her hand and led her to the living room. His floors were dark tiled with black leather couches. Next to the couch was a bottle of wine. Sophia examined the bottle and was trying to think of ways to say "no thank you" when he offered. The bottle sat in a silver urn like holder surrounded by warm water instead of ice.

"Sang Rouge?" He offered.

"Sure..." She said uncertain of what she just agreed to.

He loosened the cork on the bottle and a familiar sweet penny-like smell crept from its neck.

"Blood…"

Sophia sprang up from the couch. "WHO ARE YOU?!"

"Sophia, calm down, please!" "Sit, let me explain."

"No!"

Sophia ran to the front door at a speed that made her frame look like a blur to the human eye. She was surprised when he got to the door before her. His hand was holding the door shut and her hand was pulling at the door handle, both panting out of breath from the sprint.

He looked into her eyes hers shining a neon fierce green, his golden umber and in the center two long black slits like a python.

"Please, let me explain Sophy."

————————————

"So, what is he?" Mia tried to sound lighthearted about the news. She even sounded a little like Emily in her questioning.

"You wouldn't believe me if I told you."

"I mean... I would. We're here right. There's bound to be other creatures out there."

"Yeah but you worry too much. I'd rather you meet him first before focusing on that."

"I worry because I want nothing to happen to you or us. I want your happiness just as much, Sophia."
"Are there more of his kind?"

"Yeah, sort of. He's kind of hiding out for now. In the way that a dignitary would hideout."

"Like exile?"

"No. Anyways he's 'out of this world' as the kids say." She laughed.

"HEY! Let's go on a HUNT!" Giddily Emily screamed from the kitchen. Distracting Mia from pressing the issue of Sophia's new love.

"Wait..."

Mia looked down at her phone 3 missed calls and 8 text messages from Blaine.

1st Missed Voicemail from Blaine Abbott (12AM):

Hey Babe, hope you're having a great time with your family. Me and Phil went out to the bar and I'm just getting back now Just wanted to call and say goodnight. I miss you.

There was a sudden loud crash in the background that sounded like a tree splitting in half.

Oh shit! Babe, something just sounded like a train wreck outside. I'll call you back. Love you.

2nd Missed Voicemail from Blaine Abbott (12:37AM):

Babe… there's something wrong... I feel weird, sick to my stomach.

Umm.. it's almost 2am here and Mr. Tolstoy is outside. I haven't… haven't spoken to him in a long time. Why would he just show up?

"Hey man, were you in a crash? What are you doin' all the way out here this late...?"

"Hey Boyo, could you let me in?"

Mia listened in horror as Mr. Tolstoy's voice fluctuated between the sweet old man she knew and Mike's voice.

I think I had one too many. I thought I was fine but now I feel like I'm going to pass out. Um.. Okay, okay… he's going to help me. Mia call me ASAP.

"Just a second. Hey Mr. Tolstoy, are you okay? It's late..."

Blaine must have dropped the phone because the call kept playing in the distance. Mia could hear the garbled moans and scuffling between the two men. The last thing she heard was someone picking up the phone, a deep breath, and then the recording ended.

TEN

A NIGHT IN A RAINY TOWN

Fall 2013 - Leadville, Colorado

Michael stood under the awning in the alley behind Tolstoy's Bookshop listening to the jumbled thoughts of the man moving through the brick building.

"Her skin is so soft..."

"Her lips are so juicy…"

"I can't believe this is happening…"

Blaine's voice echoed in whispers in his mind. He cringed in disgust at his every word.

Blaine's voice whispered in Michael's mind as he heard his thoughts. His teeth ground together in a painful cringe at his every word.

Michael leaped into the air landing on the roof of the bookshop. The rain poured in sheets against him, cool dampness soaking through his jacket. He paced disgruntled before walking over to the skylight. On bent knees he watched Mia in the dimness laying on her back on a writing desk. Her skirt was bunched up around her waist. Her breasts were exposed; each perfect mound with nipples like jewels glistened with sweat under the candlelight. Her mouth opened wide; the gasps were barely audible through the rain beaten glass, but he could never forget the sound of her moans. His eyes focused on the tall young man grunting intensely in between her legs.

Michael's eyes burned as he stared at Blaine's pale mortal face. He could see his brown hair disheveled; plastered to his forehead in sweat as he continued pumping into her.

Bloody tears mixed with rain ran down Michael's face across his furled lips. His nails, now sharp claws dug jagged welts into the asphalt of the roof. He forced himself to watch her. He wanted to see if she came the same with this mortal... as she did with him. Mia's legs tightened around Blaine's waist pulling him deeper into her; Blaine leaned his head back in pure ecstasy. His veins were perfectly exposed and pulsing with heart racing blood. Even the most experienced vampire would have a hard time refusing such an opportunity to quench their thirst.

Mia sat up reaching for Blaine's neck. She nuzzled her nose across his neck feeling its warmth, smelling the sweet blood just beneath his skin, running her fingers delicately across the pulse of his veins. Michael could tell she was on the verge of biting him. She could have snapped his neck, but that's when he saw it. Michael's eyes stretched in the dark as Mia began kissing Blaine's neck. She brought his tilted head forward to hers. She closed her eyes and kissed him deeply, her hips continued to grind matching his thrusts.

Michael was raging inside. He felt like his head was going to explode when he stood up. He knew then that there was love there, not just the rough sweaty carnal pleasures they once had.

"I could have given her that... bitch." his blood was boiling, rain seeped into the creases of his tightly bald fists.

Michael sat next to the chimney letting the rain fall on his face. He didn't care that he was completely soaked. When Mia and Blaine finally laid silent, he spoke to her mind. She didn't answer. His head sank into his wet hands and when it arose, he erupted in anger. He taunted her, threatened her, hoping that her anger and maybe some fear would cause her to respond. She didn't, she ignored him. This was the first time she had not challenged him back and this made him sick to his stomach.

Footsteps on wet pavement broke Michael's rants; a pudgy old man came walking down the street. He pulled at the locked doors of the bookshop. Michael watched as Mr. Tolstoy made his way to the back-alley door; his mind rambled on about a neighbor calling to complain of the bookshop's lights still being on and possible burglars.

"Who would want to steal a book, Agnes… Blaine probably forgot to turn the lights off again." He muttered.

Michael stood above him like a great bird looking down at its prey. The old man smelled like old leather and pipe tobacco. Michael took a step off the roof drifting down into the alley, his boots splashed in a muddy puddle on the pavement. Mr. Tolstoy, startled by the splash turned around towards the dumpsters, dropping his keys next to the steps. Michael's eyes glowed a bloodshot yellow gold back at him.

He listened to the quickening irregular beat of the old man's heart as Mr. Tolstoy grabbed deep into the chest of his plaid button-down shirt. Michael ran towards him catching the old man before his head hit the cement. The rain fell into Mr. Tolstoy's face; his eyes blinking wildly like windshield wipers on an old pickup. His eyes wandered into the night sky as Michael sunk his teeth into his wrinkled neck. His feet jerked and twitched while Michael drank his essence.

In Michael's mind he saw Mr. Tolstoy's life. He drank his thoughts… on where the little safe in his office was that stored $10,000 in cash and his late wife's wedding ring, the deed to the bookshop, but most importantly Blaine's employee record with his address.

Mr. Tolstoy's neck and face became withdrawn and sunken as Michael continued to drink. His once full salt and pepper head of hair and beard became wispy and dry; his body shrank like an emptied Capri Sun pouch with nothing, but old skin and bones left. After throwing Mr. Tolstoy in the dumpster almost the same way Blaine had tossed his cigarette in there a few hours ago. Michael, picked up the wet keys from the ground, rubbed his new salt and pepper beard, then his pot belly, and practiced his best Mr. Tolstoy impression.

It was 3am when Mia noticed that Blaine was asleep. Her hand laid across his chest while her body nestled against his side, her legs were intwined around his leg. Blaine snored gently almost matching the subtle heartbeat steady under his skin.

She focused on the sounds in the room. The crackling of the dying fire, his soft snores, the howling wind, and constant rain on the roof. There was an abrupt pause in all the ambience when she heard his voice.

"I've dreamed of you Mia, where have you been my love?" Michael's voice was cold, mocking, and reverberating in her head.

Mia sat up quickly looking around the room at the dark bookshelves, her arms flew up covering her breasts.

"New York... Cali... and now Colorado. Has no place been home since you left me, my dear?"

"I was worried about you, but I see you've been busy living a mortal life."

Mia felt unnerved and vulnerable. How could he have gotten so close without her knowing.

"It takes skill, my love. Something I've developed while you were away. I have many... many talents to show you."

She grabbed Blaine's button-up putting it on, her fingers struggling with the buttons. She looked at Blaine; he smiled in his sleep and turned over, sinking deeper into the crease of the leather couch.

"I can smell him on you... like a wet dog freshly in from the rain. You smell it too. It's disgusting. Unless that's what you're into now. Animals."

"I can't wait to rip that smile right off of his face." His voice finally trailed off.

Mia stayed silent. She searched all the exits with super speed and returned to Blaine. All was secure but she knew they weren't safe, and morning was approaching soon. With the last couple of hours before dawn she cleaned up the bookshop. She felt bad leaving Blaine without explaining, but she couldn't risk his life. All she knew was that when he would awake it would be as if it all was a dream. He would wake up at the checkout desk barely remembering what had happened. Mia felt at peace in his arms something she hadn't felt in a long time and now she wasn't even sure if she would see him again.

She left the bookstore through the back alley and began her search for Michael. There was no sign of him. His scent was no longer lingering like the plague in the air. Mia retreated to her apartment on the other side of town. She drew the curtains closed on the first floor and headed downstairs to the basement where her bedroom was. There in the windowless room she lay in her bed thinking of Blaine. Michael invaded her thoughts once more.

"Talents... what talents?"

ELEVEN

THE DEVIL LAUGHS IN THE SUN

Fall 2022 - Los Angeles, California

Mia ran over to her duffel bag and searched through the pocket for her portable battery. She plugged up her phone then ran over to the closet where her sneakers sat neatly next to Emily's flats.

"I have to go... "

"Mia what's going on?" Emily walked over to her.

She sat down on the couch slipping her shoes on. She grabbed her phone and began frantically typing, booking her flight to Colorado as she spoke. "He has him."

"Who has who?!"

"Mike has Blaine! That bastard watched and waited for years! He waited until I was gone and now... I'm going to kill him if he's hurt him."

"We're coming too!" Sophia jumped up. They saw her blurred outline run up the stairs and into her room.

"Mia, WAIT the sun is coming up!" Emily yelled. The outside glowed skyline had a pale blue hue across bottom of the horizon just beneath the dark blue night sky.

"It 2am here that means it's 3am there plus an almost 3-hour flight! Full sun is right around the corner you'll never make it in time."

"I don't care! I don't have time for this! He could be dead and so help Mike if he is." She tossed her phone into the bag's pocket and zipped it firmly.

"Fuck the plane."

Mia raced out to Emily's balcony her duffel bag snug across her body, and without a thought she leaped over the metal banister into the sky. There were no visible wings like you would see in the movies. Mia's body was a clear outline passing through the clouds.

The automatic blackout curtains began to close preparing for morning light. Emily booked a flight for her and Sophia. Sophia watched the curtains block out the last of the night sky missing the daylight and Nick.

Fall 2021 - Leadville, Colorado

Mia was wind burnt when she finally landed in Leadville. She hobbled her aching body into Blaine's house. The glass in the white pine wood front door was shattered as if it was pushed back up against the wall in force.

She was exhausted after flying so quickly and on such a long journey that she collapsed at the dining room table. She knew that she had to find shelter and quickly. There was no sign or sound of Blaine. The room was bitterly cold with mountain fall air. Mia rose to her knees the table sat at eye level and upon was a letter and a squared crystal glass. The blood that filled it was congealed and cold. She fought back the urge to drink it and picked up the letter.

10/11/2022

Mia,

My love, my mistress... It's time for you to come home. You and I are alike, in power, in strength, in desire. We are elite, animals, monsters and for that we deserve each other. I know I can be... unreasonable, but that can change. I'll bend for you if you give me what I want. He will never be me, this mortal of yours, this waste of time. Let me show you. Come to me so that we may feast on his flesh together. If not, well the blood bag will die and all future blood bags or creatures you love will meet the same fate.

Mike

"Fucking ghoul!"

She crumbled the paper tightly in the palm of her fist and tossed it across the room. She could feel his toothy smile in every word. He enjoyed tormenting her and he was never going to stop. She knew that. Mia picked up the glass placing it to her nose and gave the blood a sniff. She closed her eyes and pinpointed where he was.

"Fucking sun!"

She looked at the rays coming through the curtains of the dining room windows and the open front door. She maneuvered around them making her way to the basement. There was a wine cellar that stayed dark and cool. She opened the door and went inside resting and waiting for night to fall.

Mia awoke that evening ravenously hungry with no humans in sight. That was the thing about being in the mountains, the desolateness was both a gift and a curse. She stretched her arms over her head relieving the stiffness in her joints from sleeping on the cellar floor. The basements steps creaked under her feet as she walked upstairs. The house was empty and dark. The moonlight beamed through the blinds creating rectangular spotlights on the blue shag carpet. Mia flicked on a table lamp near the couch and opened her duffel bag.

Emily Edmunds: We're here in Leadville. Let us know where you are so we can meet up.

Mia Edmunds: I'm at Blaine's place on Woodland and Forrester. Hurry!

Mia responded then plugged her phone in Blaine's charger. She held the neon blue cable in her hand for a second, not realizing how much he had meant to her until then. Maybe Michael was right, maybe they were just monsters. She grabbed her clothes from the duffel bag and headed to the shower.

By the time she was showered and dressed Emily and Sophia were standing at the open front door. When she invited them in she was surprised to see a man with dreads tied in a bun behind Sophia.

Mia bared her teeth in a growl.

"Who is that? I am not in the mood for surprise guests!" she charged towards him, but he remained standing proud beside Sophia.

"Nicholas Richardson, and he's with me, M."

"Sophy, we don't have time for this! Get this mortal out of here!"

"Mia, we can hold our own."

"Show them, Nick."

A brisk wind blew through the night forest full of green pine and yellowed leaf trees. The animals and bugs came to a serene quietness. Deathly still except for that gentle blowing of the wind. Nick's eyes were closed, his arms stretched out facing the forest. A low rustling across the ground grew louder and louder approaching them from all directions of the forest. Quickly, hundreds of the world's deadliest snakes slithered around Nick's feet. Nick began ripping off his shirt and pants, his body stretching from 6'2 to 9ft in a matter of minutes. His dark brown skin shed from his frame and disintegrated as it met the graveled walkway. The snakes continued to circle faster around his feet, some stood at attention around the pit their eyes mesmerizingly fixed.

Nick's skin rippled and stretched, hardening into cobra scales of brown, gold, and black. The lengths of his arms were encrusted with circular rubies of all sizes from his shoulders to his wrists in a neat row. His long dreads that once were tied in a neat bun cascaded down his long back these ends replaced by the heads of miniature black snacks. He opened his eyes staring through black diamond shaped pupils at the ladies; his golden irises reflecting in the moon.

Emily's mouth was open the entire transformation.

"Sophia, what the hell is that!?" Mia demanded.

"A Reptilian Prince from the planet Elyria." Sophia did a playful skip around him. She was so matter of fact about it that Mia and Emily just stared at her in amazement.

"Oh come on! So he's an alien? There are aliens now?!" Emily was stunned.

"From Elyria... It's a hidden planet near Mars. It's a little bigger than Earth, but they have a brilliant cloaking system so we wouldn't have known it existed." Sophia continued staring at Mia and ignoring Emily.

"We don't have time for surprises. Is he in control of himself? Does he know who we are?"

"Yeah, watch!"

Sophia stepped towards him, and the girls' fangs jolted out in a defensive stance. She placed her hands around his scaly waist and looked up into his serpent eyes. He looked down at them with a low hiss. She levitated a few feet above the ground, and he bent over meeting her face. She smiled at him coyly before planting a long kiss on his scaled lips.

Emily squinted her eyes at them both then at Nick.
"Where's his dick?" Emily laughed.

"Emily!" Mia scoffed."

The branches cracked under their feet. Tucked within the brush, several snakes continued to slither alongside Nick, their bellies sidewinding with his every step.

"This place smells new."

They reached the center of the woods and stood within the tree line staring at a black oak cabin. Its modern three floors were staggered on top of each other like giant steps surrounded by the dark forest. The moonlight continued to peek through the tree branches casting an ominous shadow on the cabin; one that made the edges of the rectangular structure look sharp and deadly.

Warm light illuminated under the curtains of its large, squared windows.

"He's here." Sophia said. "That bastard... I can smell him." She looked toward Nick.

"Okay, you guys find Blaine and I'll distract him." "Sophia, for once please don't let your anger get the better of you... You can have your revenge, but don't do anything reckless, my child."

"Sister, there are no heroes. We don't know what he's capable of. If you no longer sense me or the sun starts to come up and I'm not out, you run. Run as far as you can, and I'll find you. I'll always find you. Please tell Blaine the truth. Tell him that I'm sorry for whatever I must do to save him. Tell him that I loved him."

"Mia..." Emily walked over to her placing her arms around her neck. "This is NOT goodbye for us. But for Blaine... his heartbeat is faint, M. He doesn't have long. I'll do what I can, but Mike hid him somewhere in the woods. If his mortal life can't be saved, do you want me to turn him?"

Mia squeezed Emily tight, her lips whispered deeply into her ear.

"No…"
"I've created one too many vengeful children as it is. You don't need to follow in my footsteps."

She let go of her sister not knowing if she would see her again and headed to the front door.

Mia's knock on the front door echoed hollowly through the autumn night. She waited, expecting Michael to open the door so she could grab him by the throat, sink her claws into his neck, and demand where Blaine was. Footsteps approached behind the oak door. She could hear the heartbeat slow and calm on the other side. The metal doorknob turned, and the door cracked open. The warm light of a lamp in the entry way flooded her eyes. Blaine stood in the doorway wearing a navy sweatshirt, jeans, and Sperry sneakers.

Mia rushed into his arms; her head buried deep into his chest. She lost herself in his smell for a second before pulling away.

"Are you okay? Where is he?" she whispered franticly looking around him for Michael.

"I'm so sorry for this. I know there's a lot to explain, but we must go. NOW." Mia turned towards the door pulling his hand down the hall.

Blaine didn't budge. Instead, he pulled her close to him. He stared into her eyes and felt her impatient breath on his chin. He wrapped his arms around her waist and buried his lips in her neck.

"We can't, we have to go, seriously! You're in danger." She wiggled around in his grasp. "Ow! That's too tight." His hug was starting to hurt.

Mia stopped struggling and focused on his eyes. Blaine's arms had become rigid, he had stopped moving as if he was frozen in time. His eyes stared firmly at the door. The door slammed behind Mia with a gust of wind startling her. She craned her neck to see but couldn't. When she looked back at Blaine she was struck with horror. The beige softness of Blaine's cheek and jaw were melting down his sweatshirt like candle wax. Mia wrestled to break free from his arms with all her vampiric power but couldn't. He growled and screamed as his skin peeled away from the muscles and tissues in his face as his bone structure beneath began to reshape. Mia wanted to scream, and she opened her mouth too, but the sound wouldn't escape her vocal cords. Blood colored slime and flesh dripped around their feet and down the front of her body, she closed her eyes hoping that someone would come for her.

"Surprise!" Michael stood before her arms still wrapped around her waist. He placed a playful peck on her nose.

"Did you like it? It's one of my many new talents. With just an ounce of blood I can be anyone you want." He smiled down at her, his body now able to move freely.

Mia attempted again, using all her energy to get away. This time she hurled him across the room into the dining room wall.

She turned around and ran for the door in a blur, clawing at the metal knob. When she finally opened the door, she was met by long tubed metal bars. Her hands gripped both sides as she attempted to bend them, but she couldn't. She turned around to find Michael standing with his arms folded.

"Reinforced titanium. Every door, every window. Metal paneling in the walls, with unbreakable, shatterproof glass windows... Scratch free too now that cost extra." he laughed.

"Why are you doing this?"

"I missed you and wanted to talk."

"So, you kidnap a human and me just to talk. Sounds a little desperate..."

"Well, yes and no. I kidnapped the mortal because it was fun. They're so fragile you know."

"Let him go Mike."

"He is going... Don't you hear it the slowing of his meaningless little heartbeat..." he placed his hand to his ear mockingly listening to the air. "Oh wait, I don't hear anything... Sounds like he's already gone." he laughed.

Mia turned around grabbing the bars, her screams could be heard throughout the forest, yet no one came, not even Emily.

TWELVE

ONE LAST THRILL TO KILL

Fall 2022 – Mount Elbert, Colorado

"Let's spare ourselves the long-drawn-out argument that we usually have, Michael. I came here for Blaine, where is he?"

"Looking a little sun-kissed, my love. You, of all vampires with your innocent face and callous heart... risked death by the sun for a missing mortal? Somehow, I doubt that... you missed me didn't you?"

She remained silent as he continued his rant pacing back and forth in front of the bar.

"What we have… is not for the weak. We are powerful together. This one mortal with his aging skin and graying hair will soon be dust and we will continue to transcend beyond his existence. He'll be a piece of dust on your memory, and you'll have no one to share eternity with but me. No one who wants you as badly as… as I always will…"

Michael reached for her chin, caressing its soft curve. His touch sent tingles across her neck and up her back before she stepped away from him.

Mia looked around at her new prison, a large dial clock stared back at her from the living room counting down the minutes until dawn. It was a minimalist modern four-bedroom cabin, all dark brown wood except for the pine floors. A grand piano sat nestled next to a marble fireplace, its pristine ivory and black lacquer keys felt cold under her fingertips. This would have been a beautiful place to be if it weren't for the reinforced metal and her captor. Michael always knew what she liked, and how to set the stage for his conquest. She wanted to fight him, but there was a part of her that knew he was right. Mia needed to leave, but she wanted to stay.

She loved Blaine, his fragility, how he lived every day with the fullest intention because tomorrow would be a day closer to his death. The longer she thought about it the more she hated how right Mike was, how he made her question her loyalty that should have been unwavering. Sure, she didn't have any intentions to turn him, but that didn't mean she loved him any less, or did it?

With Michael life was one endless night, one great party. There was always excitement, but at cost, trauma… regret… He was a long-winded run-on sentence when he felt he was right about something, but he challenged her. He always matched her power, her energy, her anger, and with that he was her favorite of lovers. The tone of her voice in her mind was cold and careless.

There are two sides to every person. It's a constant battle between the light and the dark. Most days we try to stay in the light… But sometimes you let the light side take a blow to the face so the dark side can flourish. This is one of those nights. Say goodnight, to the light.

"My love are you here with me or is your mind with him?" Michael's voice brought her back to the present.

Mia felt the light bulb that she worked so hard to keep shining brightly in her heart flick off. She heard the sound of a dusty gold lighter, its cold metal stricken to light the wick of an old wax candle, one that slowly brightened in the dark corner of her soul.

"I'm here... I was thinking about what you just said, fleeting years and all... you're right Mike."

Mia hated it, but he always awakened a part of her as if under a spell. She still had to give the girls and Nick time to find Blaine and get him to safety, but she knew their relationship would be over once this night ended. She could never be with Blaine, but she could never be with Michael either. And Michael would never stop hunting her.

"I'm not stupid, Mia. Don't think that you can just come in here telling me I'm right and that's going to save him."

"No, Mikey you are right. No sarcasm attached. What happens to him is no longer my concern. Now what is it you want to talk about?" Mia walked towards him. She got to see the crater she created throwing him into the wall a little more clearly, the force he withstood. Her body tingled once more as her panties felt a familiar wetness, a wetness she missed dearly.

THIRTEEN

———

BLAINE'S DEAD

Once Sophia and Nick were out of sight the silence broke into a melodic musical of crickets chirping and the wind rustling through the leaves. Emily concentrated her mind moving through the mysterious sounds of nature's nightlife to listen for Blaine's seldom heartbeat. An owl hooted in the distance as she walked up a small hill in the darkness, leaves and branches crunching under her white muddied sneakers. She tracked his heartbeat again and this time it sounded like the drip from a leaky faucet. She closed her eyes to see it better, her ears sending invisible waves through the trees until they reverberated on soft flesh sitting against the bottom of a large old tree.

She flew through the treetops approaching the tree from its back side. Emily would follow her sister's directions, if he was too far gone, she would stay with him until he passed instead of turning him into one of them. If he was okay, she would fly him to safety, get him whatever help he needed, and when he finally recovered, she would tell him the truth. She was about 100ft away when she could hear him gurgling as he choked on his own blood, but there was something else, a wince of pain, a small cry out and then a second voice that moaned deeply in ecstasy and fulfillment.

Nick stood across from Sophia watching her drain the last drops of Blaine's blood from the two puncture wounds in his neck. He watched betrayal unfold, but even then, remained loyal to her. Emily pulled Sophia off of Blaine, the front of his shirt was torn and soaked in his own blood.

"What the fuck, Sophia?! Have you lost the little bit of sense I thought you had!" Emily couldn't contain her rage. "I was at your side every step of the way, even when she left. Do you understand what you have fucking done to us?"

Sophia's olive face, now flushed with rosy, red cheeks from fresh blood stared emotionlessly at Emily while walking past her in a daze over to Nick's side.

"How dare you disrespect me! I raised you, guided you, you ungrateful bitch! Mia should have left you on that bathroom floor where you belonged! If you think you got some kind of revenge, you didn't. This was weak because YOU are weak."

Emily lunged on top of Sophia, clawing at her throat and face. She ripped through muscles and tissues before a firm scaled hand grabbed her shoulder, flinging her into the body of the old tree just above Blaine's head. Her torso took the full impact of the blow as the giant pine snapped in two. Emily, the once old and powerful vampire now cried out in excruciating pain, crawling on her belly across the dirt in the direction of the cabin.

"Mia... MIA!" she screamed in the darkness. The night sky was spinning above her. She focused on the misty clouds of stars that seemed to spiral down upon them. Nick stood above her blocking out the swirls. The weight of his body overpowered her as he sank his serpent fangs into her collar bone. The bones beneath the skin shattered into little fragments from the pressure as he injected his venom into her neck.

He never spoke a word, never yelled, or growled. Nick was completely serene in his choice to protect Sophia.

Emily's veins began to bulge and pulse throughout her body. Her eyes became a bloodshot red and then a deep burgundy to black as if they were melting out of her skull. Blood ran across her cheeks from her eyes and veins, now blackened and burned. Her body convulsed under his grip.

"Nick! STOP!" Sophia commanded. He retreated almost immediately.

Sophia bent down, hovering over Emily's body listening to her violent gasps that escaped her cracked dark lips. Emily listened intently for any sound. The stars she had once seen became a fog of blackness. She could not hear or see anymore as white venom continued to ooze from her eyes, mouth, ears, and the puncture on her neck.

"My dear Aunt Emily..."

"Rest well." Sophia's voice was cold and confused although Emily never heard her words.

She kissed Emily on her motionless lips, the venom now drying into flaked crusts around her mouth. Nick's hand met Sophia's as the sky began to show a twilight morning blue. They vanished in the forest leaving her to die alongside Blaine's bloody corpse. She never heard Mia's scream, and Mia never heard hers.

———————————

Her fingers played the keys on the piano, a gentle tune that reminded her of the old country with her sister. If she were to succumb to daylight, she would have only wanted her in her mind. Plus, it was the only melody she knew how to play on the piano. Each digit landing on the cool ivory keys. Michael walked over to her caressing the top of her hand.

"I wanted to talk about us…"

"Well as far as I knew there was no 'us'. You made that clear." Mia never raised her head to look at him. She focused on the piano and the fog that was forming on the edges of the large windows from the heat in the room.

"I was arrogant, reckless, yes. But you can't say I didn't care for you."

"You didn't." Her words were sharp as if she threw a dagger at him although she didn't intend to project so much feeling.

"I always will, Mia. You need to stop making up that I hated you."

"It's what it felt like."

Michael's hand caressed up the back of her neck, his fingers interlaced between her hair. He grabbed a handful, tilting her head up and to the side exposing her soft, slender neck. Mia winced at his grip, feeling the strain underneath her jaw and neck. She liked the pain as she smiled sinisterly, her tongue traced the plumpness of her bottom lip. She sucked in a corner of the plump flesh and bit down tasting little beads of her own blood.

His pointer finger turned her face to the side at a speed that would have snapped the neck of a mortal, his thumb plunged into the dip under her jaw. He trailed kisses from her collar bone to her jawline, deep and savory with strength and pressure. His thumb caressed down the front of her throat feeling each indentation of smooth cartilage under her cocoa skin.

"Just... Mia, let me touch you. Worship you... your power, your ferocity. I know what you think of me but let me just do this. You didn't come back for him... You came back for this... for me." He whispered into her lips; his eyes locked on to hers. He knew her soul, the guttery, gritty, fleshy parts of it.

Michael's hand loosened around her throat, his roughened fingers trailing down the softness of her neck to the middle of her breasts. He placed the palm of his hand against her heart knowing there would be no blood flowing through the arteries of that muscle deep within. Its silence was hollow, but he still imagined the feeling of a steady percussion of pulse that quickened at his touch.

He wanted her soul. She was always more passionate when he broke her. She loved him a little more each time like a prisoner falling in love with her captor. Maybe if she broke just enough, she could love him past the monster that he was. He wanted control of her passion for him which took emotion, emotion he never wanted to admit he had. He barely wanted to admit to himself that he was changing.

Mia's lips were pursed together tightly waiting for his hand to move. He brought his fingers back to her lips, his thumb running across the slit until she released the breath she was holding. He listened to her sigh, that familiar 'maybe he has changed' sigh. He didn't want her softness nor her love. He didn't want to become another Blaine in her life. Michael wanted to be the igniter of her passion, the reason why she used a vibrator after being thrusted into by her mortal lover and him not being enough.

He traced the outline of her hips then reached down the front of her jeans roughly pulling her panties away and thrusting his fingers in between her lips. His digits slipped between the wet folds. "See Mia, you're wet for me."

Mia fell against his hand, her body leaning against his, her legs wrapped tightly together around his arm. She wanted to move away, but her body was giving in. Mia felt the weakness in the muscles of her thighs becoming weaker with every flick of his finger on her clit.

"Oh, the confidence you fucking have, narcissist. You don't fucking deserve me, Michael." Mia spoke through gritted teeth. Her moans of each syllable lingered in his ear.

"Strip." he directed.

Mia pulled her shirt over her head and took off her jeans remaining in her sheer navy-blue bra and panties.

"I said strip." he grabbed another handful of her hair jolting her face towards his. He loved how it felt in between his fingers and palm.

He removed his leather belt from his pants, wrapping it around his hand. He unzipped his pant, reached inside, and pulled out his dick. Its veins pulsed under the beige skin. He placed it on her chin just below the curl of her bottom lip and without words she took the length of him into her mouth. His legs almost gave out from the feeling as his eyes closed tightly and he let out a growl that echoed amongst the wooden beams in the ceiling.

Mia's pussy quivered with each thrust into her throat. Its pink lips glistening with her sweet wetness, vibrating in anticipation of his touch. The room smelled of her passion and Michael inhaled deeply with each stroke against her tongue.

"You deserve everything I'm about to give you, and more." He made a point to stare into her eyes before he said to her. "I see you, Mia."

He bit down firmly into her shoulder, her blood pouring into his mouth. When he drew his head back, he watched as the two puncture marks healed almost instantly. Their lips locked in a passionate kiss as they spun violently in the air, two cyclones of animalistic pleasure being their total selves without regret. Mia sank her teeth into his chest while his claws ripped at her back and torso. His blood flowed into her mouth like the smoothest tasting Pinot noir you could never afford. A blood bonding, she thought to herself, in other words a sacrifice.

"Whatever powers he has I'll have, wherever he is I'll know, but the exchange is he will always find me. In every lifetime, no matter how far, no matter what world."

Her head tilted back, fangs fully erect and dripping with his blood. Her cute, pointed nose had become short and drawn into her face, her ears were pointed, and her hands and legs now a mix of humanoid and bat appendages grew fine hairs. Her body was fuzzed all except for her breast and stomach that still shown a deep rich brown flesh that stood firm and supple. Her face was still beautiful, but her ebony cheeks now chiseled and tight became more of the beast she knew she was.

"See, don't you feel better? Not having to be anyone else but yourself and being able to share that gift with someone who loves both sides of you." Michael gestured to her dark form before he himself fully transformed.

"You don't love me; you only love yourself. You love the thrill of this chase and so do I. Nothing more, nothing less. Don't try to pretend this is a fairytale so that I can feel something for you. You're constant, predictable, and you'll always answer when I text or call. That's not love, that's obedience."

Michael squinted his eyes, he knew she was right, but also, she was intentionally making him angry. The angrier he would get the better the sex was.

She hated that she was addicted to him… to this… his touch. That at an instant he could make all the hate she felt for him disappear with a word or a gesture. This was just another reason why she stayed away.

———————————

Sophia and Nick stood outside the cabin listening to the moans and growls from Michael and Mia. Sophia was enraged as tears of blood streamed down her face.

"That lying bitch!"

She was no longer sorry about Emily; she wasn't sorry about Blaine. She wanted both to suffer and if they all died including her, she no longer cared.

"Babe, tear them limb from limb."

Nick leaped onto the roof of the cabin tearing a gigantic hole through the wood and metal. Large sheets of rubble landed on top of and around Michael and Mia. Mia received the worst of the blow knocking her unconscious.

Michael's mouth was agape while staring at the 9ft reptilian man. "Oh well that's new" he said while quickly putting on his pants. Sophia entered through the opening in the roof. The look of disgust on her face was painful as the tears of blood ran heavier and faster down her cheeks. There was no conversation before Nick began to strike.

"Well, you sure have grown up Sophia. How's the family? Oh wait, sorry. I almost forgot." He smiled at her lighting a cigarette and tipping the ash towards her.

The embers of gray and white drifted feathery onto the wood floor as Nick's claws landed across Michael's face.3

Sophia watched as Nick and Michael battled across the room, on each wall, on every ceiling. She could see as Michael gritted his teeth that he was trying his hardest not to give in to defeat.

With every slice of his flesh from Nick's claws Michael regenerated slower and slower, his skin turned a pale green like Emily's. He lasted 20 more minutes before collapsing to the floor. Mia still laid naked and unconscious around the room while Nick's mouth stretched wide and bit down entirely on Mike's head. His headless body fell next to the couch blood spewing from his open neck.

FOURTEEN

MIDNIGHT SUN

Mia's naked body lay beside the rubble and in her unconsciousness, she dreamed of her human days in the old country. Malay and Salma Hasina stood on the banks of the Moulouya River. The hot sun touched their foreheads and breasts creating beads of sweat. This was a regular occurrence for the sisters of the Kingdom of Numidia 238 BC. The sun always seemed close to them at that point. Even in the desert storms of Northern Africa the air was crisper then.

Malay and Salma were the daughter of the local high priestess, Zara and would always be found by the river side collecting herbs and flowers for Zara for medicines and potions. Malay was 23 years old and not yet married. She thought marriage was boring and although the king wanted his son to be betrothed to her, she often evaded the conversation by bringing up a local invention or her mother's newest healing concoction. Salma, her sister was 20 years old and always timid. She was an open thinker always staring at the clouds and flamingos that were wading in the water looking for food to eat. Everyone in the tribe had their thoughts about the family, but one attribute that was always mentioned especially by men was that the women of the Hasina family were beautiful. Malay's skin was a deep cocoa brown and Salma was a rich caramel. Salma resembled their great grandma Shala with her honey-colored eyes and fairer skin. Malay was the exact image of her mother Zara in her youth.

After the gathering of marigolds and herbs for their mother's medicinal powders the sisters set their pouches aside and bathed in the river just offshore. The calming movement as the sun beams glittered on its ripples turning the muddy brown waters to waves of golden hues. They waded in its coolness before gathering their things and heading home.

That night Malay stood by her mother at the fireplace as she mixed the herbs that they had found earlier in the day. The shadow of her mother's arm stirring the caldron above the fire was mesmerizing. The spell had been broken when their front door was kicked in. The dust from the dirt floor rose and when it cleared there stood 5 men in robes with torches. Malay ran to the other side of the room grabbing Salma and huddled behind a chair and the wall. The men were yelling and pointing at their mother, seething, and foaming from the mouth with anger. One of the men walked over slapping Zara to the ground. Zara let out a wailing scream unlike any noise her daughters had ever heard her make. She struggled and fought as two other men grabbed her ankles and wrists sliding her across the floor and out the door. Zara's headwrap disheveled, dragged behind her exposing her long dark brown locks.

An older man, calm and detached from the mob stood in their door frame staring at the girls while watching the torture. Malay never broke eye contact with him as he stood there. She knew that if he came for them, she would cut him into ribbons with the knife that her mother left on the kitchen table. She felt that although he had a straight face he was grinning sinisterly behind his lips.

Outside the house the white men in robes of vibrant reds and golds stood with raised torches. The priests of the local Catholic church formed a circle around Zara each armed with medium sized stones in a pouch. With each yell they picked out a rock from the pouch and hurdled it at Zara's head and body. The bruises and blood were immediate on her bronzed skin. Her screams of agony were deafening as they stripped her down to her cream-colored gown. Her lips were busted, and her eyes blackened.

Malay held Salma close to her covering her eyes and ears while their mother was stoned to death.

Zara's dress once beautiful oranges, golds, and purples was now a deep shade of burgundy. A mixture of blood and sand was caked into her busted lips and eyes were swollen as she laid breathing her last breaths. The girls were in shock as the men backed away from their mother and headed towards them. The man who stood at the door was still quiet as if he was in another place. He stepped Infront of the door blocking the entryway from the men and in a low tone, barely a whisper, he commanded the men to head back on their horses to town.

The man returned to the girls this time walking towards the fireplace. He was mesmerized by the unattended caldron that was now boiling over and spilling onto the open flames.

"Sit child, I can tell you are the braver of the two of you, sit." He spoke as if directly into Malay's mind. She never saw his lips move.

Hesitant with tears of rage stinging her eyes she stood up and walked to the chair almost as if she was being controlled. Salma clung to the bottom of her dress sobbing uncontrollably. She focused on the roughness of the wood on the back of her legs as he spoke to her.

"My name is Edmund, child."

"There are no children here." Malay spat.

"Well you are to me. A powerful one at that. I felt your energy this morning at the river. It almost blew me out of the ground."

"Out of the ground..."

"Nevermind that, I come to bring you a gift. That's if you want it."

Malay sat silent; her eyes moved to the door where she could see the foot of her mother lying still. Fresh tears rolled down her face and chin.

"I can take you away from here and give you riches you could only dream of. Also, the revenge I know you now seek." Edmund told her.

"Those men will come back. And soon. You won't be ready to take them on, but with my gift and guidance you'll be the most powerful woman in the world."

Malay looked at her sister's scared blubbering face. Salma was strong and to see her this vulnerable was even more heartbreaking. Those men stole their lives and it was up to her to get it back.

"So what will it be, Malay?" Edmund broke into Malay's thoughts.

"And what of my sister, will she get this gift too?"

"If you wish it. She is quite powerful as well. Right, Salma?"

Salma's head lifted to meet his gaze. She looked at Malay and shook her head.

Malay nodded at Edmund in agreement and that was the last night of their mortal lives and the last night they saw Edmund.

———————————

The pale sun beamed across Mia's back from the opening in the cabin's roof when she finally regained consciousness. In her daze she removed the rubble from off of her dirty naked body. Her arms and legs were back to their slender human shape. She hadn't thought of Edmund in a long time, but he flooded her thoughts as if he was standing in the room with her. She could smell the fall leaves, big trees rustling oranges and yellows as wind crept through its branches. She stood up staring into the sky directly into the sun until it became a black dot within the blue clouds.

"THE SUN!" Mia scrambled on weakened legs for the nearest place to hide, but quickly found there was nowhere that she could go from the light. She looked at the front door and the bars that once locked her in were gone. Michael was gone. And most of her memories from last night were gone.

———————————

There was a digging of earth next to Emily. She couldn't hear or see, but she could feel the disruption next to her. Frozen in her poisoned body she accepted that she would either be burned by the sun in the next couple of hours or the rest of her would be eaten by a hungry animal.

Emily felt her body lifted and placed into a hole, the cool earth beneath her was welcomed, relieving the fever she felt inside. Warm liquid dripped over her cracked lips, a familiar taste. She drank until the greenish grey color was gone from her skin returning it back to its bronze glow. The first shovel of dirt on top of her body was the scariest, but then she realized this was someone who cared for her. The taste lingered in her mouth until a memory formed crystal blue eyes.

Greyson.

———————————

Michael's body was buried deep in the Colorado woods. He laid motionless in the unmarked grave. Sophia wept for her human family above the grave, her bloody tears poured through her hands to the ground. There would never be another baby, another Richard, and the pain she thought would end after she got her revenge wasn't sated. She looked at Nick through blood-stained eyes and could feel there was a change in him. He was judging her actions and he knew that she used him.

Nick's scales began to shed as the morning sun hit them. His height returned to his human size and his dreads were no longer snakes. He stood in the old shower of a hotel in downtown Colorado, the water cascading down his back while Sophia slept in her coffin.

He grabbed the metal handle to turn the water as hot as possible. The steam rose above him fogging up the windows and mirror. He ran his hand through his long mane letting out a sigh, blood ran into the drain, a mixture of Emily and Michael's blood as he washed himself. Towards the end he stood there, staring out through the opening of the shower curtain at the coffin.

Sophia couldn't be trusted. Her rage was able to control him, and he wasn't sure how, but he knew she could be dangerous to him, and people like him. He contemplated what he would do and once he was done showering, he decided that he would take her back to Elyria as his lover and his experiment on the vampire race for the safety of his people, the ones he regretfully abandoned.

EPIPILOGUE

———

"Candace, my dear. Wake up…"

"Wake up…" A male's voice drifted across Candace's lips and forehead like a careful hand.

Candace sat with her knees to her chest as the shower down poured scalding hot water onto her scalp and back. The California moonlight shined in the window through a crack in the newspaper she had haphazardly placed when she realized the sun was no longer her friend. Candace had fallen asleep in a position she had become comfortable with ever since her incident in 2002 at Lucky's Laundromat. The water drowned out her own thoughts and calmed her.

Candace's bloody fingertips from her last kill created long lines of pink and red down her tanned legs, swirling like the lines on a peppermint into the open drain. She sobbed thinking about the matted blood in her curly hair and on her face.

The vibration of her iPhone, still broken from the fight, caused her to jump. Her phone cast a dimmed light in the corner of the bathroom stinging her eyes. She squinted trying to make out who it is calling, the dried blood cracking along the creases of her eyes.

Nicole's face continued to appear. She whimpered remembering seeing that exact face appeared on her phone when she had finally come to the night she was attacked.

"My child, stop pitying yourself. You've been reborn, be grateful. Now get up, we have work to do. Come find me in Colorado. It won't be easy, but I'm there." The voice was loud and angry, but mesmerizing, she grabbed her towel, put on her jeans with a light blue crop top and headed for the door.

Michael's voice continued until he trailed off in her mind...

Thank you so much for reading!

Stay tuned for VOL. II!